We hope you enjoy this book. Please return or renew it by the due date.

You can renew it at www.norfolk.gov.uk/libraries or by using our free library app.

Otherwise you can phone 0344 800 8020 - please have your library card and PIN rea

You can sign up for email reminders too

NORFOLK ITEM

30129 082 139 578

NORFOLK COUNTY COUNCIL
LIBRARY AND INFORMATION SERVICE

VERDICT
OF TWELVE

RAYMOND POSTGATE

With an Introduction by
MARTIN EDWARDS

This edition published 2017 by
The British Library
96 Euston Road
London
NW1 2DB

Originally published in 1940 by Collins

Copyright © 2017 Estate of Raymond Postgate
Introduction copyright © 2017 Martin Edwards

Cataloguing in Publication Data
A catalogue record for this publication is
available from the British Library

ISBN 978 0 7123 5674 9

Typeset by Tetragon, London
Printed and bound by
CPI Group (UK) Ltd, Croydon CR0 4YY

CONTENTS

INTRODUCTION

Verdict of Twelve is so often cited as a classic of crime fiction that it is hard to believe that it is has languished out of sight for decades. This British Library Crime Classics edition puts an end to the years of bewildering neglect, and offers a new generation of readers the chance to find out why so many leading commentators have admired this novel for so long.

Raymond Chandler praised this "ironic study" of the workings of a jury in his famous essay "The Simple Art of Murder", while the eminent critic Julian Symons included the book in his list of the one hundred "best" crime novels. I first came across *Verdict of Twelve* as a schoolboy, when it appeared in an excellent series of reprinted "Classics of Detection and Adventure" selected and introduced by Michael Gilbert. His enthusiasm for the book was infectious—he went so far as to suggest that it was the "single, shining exception" to the general proposition that detective novels written by dabblers in the genre, including such distinguished authors as E.C. Bentley and A.A. Milne, had failed to stand the test of time.

Like Gilbert, I have been a solicitor as well as a crime novelist, and I share his admiration for the skill with which Raymond Postgate handles his innovative account of a murder trial. Gilbert acknowledged that Postgate's lawyers (unlike the jurors) are only caricatures, and that it was debatable whether the case would have been brought to trial, but felt that the account of "the *machinery* of the law in action" was splendid. Re-reading Gilbert's introduction more than thirty years after I first enjoyed it, I now realize that it contains a number of tiny factual errors; but these do not matter, so persuasive is his advocacy on behalf of the book. In the same way, we can allow Postgate some latitude in his presentation of the case, because his story is so compelling.

The story is crammed, as Gilbert said, with shrewd touches, many of which are to be found in his fascinating pen-portraits of the jurors. Postgate presents us with a mystery with a difference; to quote Gilbert: "I am by no means convinced that a reader would be any worse off if he did read the last page of the book first. It could be argues that what he lost on the swings of suspense, he gained on the roundabouts of psychological understanding." Having read the book four times, I entirely agree.

Julian Symons said that *Verdict of Twelve* was the best book written under the influence of Francis Iles (the pen-name under which Anthony Berkeley published two ambitious novels about criminal psychology, *Malice Aforethought* and *Before the Fact*). The ironic and cynical flavour of the Iles books inspired talented writers such as Anthony Rolls (the pen-name of C.E. Vulliamy), Bruce Hamilton, and Richard Hull.

Interestingly, Hull's *Excellent Intentions* anticipates *Verdict of Twelve* to an extent in providing an insight into shifting attitudes in the confines of the jury room. And as if to prove that there is nothing new under the sun, an even earlier book, *The Jury Disagree*, by George Goodchild and C.E. Bechofer Roberts (1934) offers another intriguing variation on this concept. Each of the three books is distinctive and worth reading on its own merits.

The epigraph to *Verdict of Twelve* comes from Karl Marx, a clue to where Raymond Postgate's political sympathies lay.

Postgate (1896–1971), the son of a professor, came from a wealthy family, and studied at St. John's College, Oxford, but he rebelled against his father's conservatism. After becoming a pacifist, he served a brief prison sentence for refusing to be conscripted; in 1920 he joined the Communist Party of Great Britain, although he deserted it two years later in favour of the Labour Party. His wife Daisy was the daughter of George Lansbury, who led Labour from 1932–5. Postgate became a successful journalist, and was editor of the socialist weekly *Tribune* at the time this book was published. His political awareness is reflected in the sharp insight into the ugliness of anti-Semitism evident in his presentation of Alice Morris's bleak story, even if modern writers might make similar points using different language.

Raymond's sister Margaret married the left-wing economist G.D.H. Cole. She and her husband wrote a long series of detective novels together that won many admirers during "the Golden Age of murder" between the wars, and the couple became members of the Detection Club, which Anthony Berkeley founded in 1930. Margaret occasionally reviewed detective fiction, but none of the Coles' books match the flair of *Verdict of Twelve*. Raymond and his brother-in-law held similar political beliefs, and they co-authored *The Common People* (1938), a social history of Britain from the mid-eighteenth century.

As a crime writer, Postgate was, essentially, a one-hit wonder. His two later mysteries, *Somebody at the Door* and *The Ledger is Kept* were interesting, but made so little impact that Michael Gilbert was not even aware of them. In the 1950s, Postgate abandoned the genre for good. He was a gourmand, and his campaign for better catering in the UK led to his founding the Good Food Club (his original name for it was the Society for the Prevention of Cruelty to Food). In 1951, he compiled the first edition of *The Good Food Guide*, now a national institution, and he proceeded to supervise the Guide "as President and Editor" until almost the end of his life. Perhaps he could fairly be described as a caviar socialist.

Postgate's son, Oliver, became a highly successful creator and writer of children's television programmes, such as *Ivor the Engine*, *Clangers*, and *Bagpuss*. Professor Yaffle in *Bagpuss* bears a distinct resemblance to Oliver's gifted but humourless uncle, G.D.H. Cole—and so, in some respects, does Dr. Percival Holmes, in *Verdict of Twelve*. Whether any of the other jurors in the novel were inspired by real life, I do not know. What is beyond doubt is that Postgate brings them to life with brilliant economy. The characterization of the people in the story, as well as the teasing mystery, and the dark cynicism about human behaviour and the nature of justice, make this a crime novel to cherish.

MARTIN EDWARDS
www.martinedwardsbooks.com

Author's Note

Toxicologists will note an error in the middle of Part II. This is intentional, for obvious reasons. Apart from this, I am advised by expert friends that the information given is correct.

I swear by almighty God that I will well and truly try and true deliverance make between our sovereign lord the King and the prisoner at the bar whom I shall have in charge and a true verdict give according to the evidence.

JURORS' OATH IN A TRIAL FOR MURDER

It is not the consciousness of men that determines their existence, but on the contrary their social existence determines their consciousness.

K. MARX

PART I

The Jury

The Clerk of Assize had to have some way of relieving the tedium of administering the same oath year after year. His habit was to stand for nearly a minute inspecting the jury and weighing it up; then he would administer the oath rather slowly, watching each juror and trying to estimate how well he would do his work. He flattered himself he could always spot the fool or the fanatic who would hold out in a minority of one and prevent a decision.

To-day he paused as usual and looked at the row of respectable persons awaiting his instructions. Two women, one rather handsome man, two rather elderly men—nothing out of the ordinary. A very commonplace jury, he reflected. But there, for that very reason it was probably likely to do all the better. No surprises, and no strange persons on the jury meant no surprises and no freakishness when the verdict came.

He cleared his throat and turned to the first, a severe looking, very plain middle-aged woman in black, wearing glasses. "Victoria Mary Atkins," he said, "repeat after me…"

"OXFORD AND CAMBRIDGE ARE TWO DELIGHTFUL TOWNS, dominated by the Universities and retaining much of their medieval character." This is a lie, as you would know if you had lived in Coronation Street, Cambridge, as Victoria Mary Atkins did. The life of the university has, and had when she was born, nothing, nothing whatever, to do with the life of the town—not of such streets as Coronation Street, anyway. And there was nothing medieval about that unbroken line of yellow-brick little houses, flush on the street, and each one identical with the other. Except insofar as wretchedness, darkness and dirt are medieval.

Victoria was the fifth of nine children; her father died when she was eleven. He was an unskilled labourer, and no loss to any one. His wages, when in work, had averaged 21s. a week and he drank. He beat his children, and his wife, with a strap, but Victoria did not hold that against him. Being beaten was after all a natural thing to happen to any child. With a bit of sneaking and slyness you could often enough get bigger children into trouble and see your grudges avenged; an occasional sore behind yourself was a small price to pay. No; it was not the beatings which Victoria held against her father. It was the continual hunger which made her grow pinched and rickety, the shame of existing for months on relief, the worse shame of dressing in rags, and an earlier violence that she could not remember, which had resulted in one of her legs being slightly shorter than another.

Even so, father was a less dangerous enemy than mother. Father was at least away at work sometimes, and sometimes harmlessly drunk or even jolly. Mother was never away for more than a few minutes from the two rooms which were home, and was never anything but sour. Father was not "noticing"; Mother was, and what's more would twist your arm till you screamed if you sulked and wouldn't answer.

Two years after her father's death Victoria slapped her mother's face, scratched her cheek, and tripped her over the coal scuttle. She had realized that at thirteen she was probably as strong as her mother, and certainty quicker witted. While her mother was picking herself up from the scuttle, she didn't run away; fists clenched, breathing very fast and a little frightened she stood her ground.

When her mother, instead of attacking her began to scream "You wicked, wicked girl!" she knew that she had won. Henceforward she was free. One of her two elder brothers might perhaps belt her now and again, but that would be all. She could run about the streets like a dog if she chose.

But beyond petty thieving, from which she had never been discouraged, there was not much harm that an ugly little girl could come to in Cambridge in 1911. She was dirty, dressed in patches, with twisted front teeth, a limp, and a hideous slum accent. She was known to have a nasty temper. Naturally she found few companions. The freedom of the streets after a year had become a bore, and she was not really distressed (though she complained on principle) when it was suddenly ended.

Mother collapsed on the stairs one Monday morning. The ambulance fetched her away and her family was told she would never come back; in fact she died in the infirmary.

The Guardians had resented their statutory obligation to feed and care for this shiftless and overlarge family; they had evaded doing it properly as long as they could; now they could not avoid it any more. But at least they made every effort they could to put the burden elsewhere. They cajoled and bullied Aunt Ethel, a square-shaped woman of nearly forty who kept a shop in Cherry Hinton, to come down to the house with their representative, a bright and experienced woman of middle age. The two found the family, or what was left of it, under the reluctant care of a neighbour, Mrs. Elizabeth Saunders.

"And glad I am to see you," said Mrs. Saunders. "Not one minute longer will I stay with such a dirty and disagreeable lot of children. There are very few would be so Christian as to look after them as I have done, with no obligations whatever. And now you *have* come, I'll leave you with them and nothing more will I do."

Surprised at this vehemence, the Guardians' lady began to say she was sure every one was very grateful, and much appreciated all that Mrs. Saunders—but she realized she was speaking to a departing back and gave it up.

"Now, my dears," she said briskly, "your Aunt Ethel has very kindly come in from Cherry Hinton, and we must all get together and have a nice comfy talk and settle what to do while your poor Mummy is ill. I thought there would be some *older* children here," she added inquiringly. "Are you Violet?" she said to the one who appeared to be the eldest.

The girl addressed dribbled and made a kind of mooing noise.

"That's Lily," said Aunt Ethel. "Lacking. Always was. Ought to be in a 'sylum. Violet's in service in Cottenham and it's not her day off. She gets 5s. 6d. a week and lucky to get it. You won't get any help from *her*."

"Oh, I see. Dear me. Well, there's Edward—no, of course, he went away three years ago. But where's Robert?"

Victoria piped up, delighted to offer bad news. "You won't find 'im. 'E went to ve stition vis morning; saw 'im. Soon as 'e 'eard Ma was gorn 'e said 'e was off. Not going to be responsible for us lot, 'e said, not —— likely." There was a participle before the last word which is even now not widely used by young women, and the Guardians' lady and Aunt Ethel glared.

Victoria stared back: it took more than a glare to discompose her. In that moment Aunt Ethel took a resolution: she would not let that foul-mouthed child into her house. The Guardians' lady was talking to her, but she did not listen. She broke into her suggestions without ceremony.

"You'll have to take poor Lily where she belongs. You know quite well what your obligations are, miss. As for these poor orphans, I'll take these three into my home and look after them and be glad." She pointed to the three younger children—two boys and the baby May. "Victoria can't come. There's no room for her, and she's too old. She's a bad girl and a bad influence already."

Nothing would shift her from this decision, and in the end the Guardians' lady took Victoria with her, to be put in a Home.

Now a Home for Girls, even before the war, even in the provinces, was not always one of the hellholes which realistic writers will describe for you. The West Fen Home did the best that could be done for Victoria, and if it did no better it was because she came to it too late. It fed her properly for the first time in her life, gave her glasses which were approximately what her eyes needed, and provided a built-up boot for her left leg. It clothed her drably, but sufficiently and warmly. It taught her to speak correctly and modified her abominable accent. Since she had benefited scarcely at all from her interrupted attendances at the Board school it taught her properly reading, writing and arithmetic, and to read the Bible.

More than that, she was taught thoroughly the art of being a domestic servant. She could wash, clean rooms, make beds, blacklead grates, sew and do plain cooking with unsurpassed thoroughness. If drilling could make one, she was the perfect maid; moreover, she was respectful. The staff would have been kind to her as well as strict if she had responded to kindness; as she did not, it was satisfied by her covering up with an impassive and silent manner her undiminished bad temper and spite. It would have been very surprised to know her real opinion both of itself and of the rare adults from outside whom she met.

In 1915 it sent her out from the Home into a good position with the wife of a don. She kept her place for six months and left, with an excellent reference, to go into munitions. She moved to London and saved all that she could; by the end of the war, when the factory closed down, she had just over £200. She was parsimonious, had few friends, and dressed always in black: she was not attractive, but after the war mistresses could not be too particular. Servants were too rare. A girl with such excellent references and so universally competent about the house was a treasure; and at least there would be no trouble with "followers". All the same Victoria did not keep her situations long. One she left under a strong suspicion of stealing, though when her mistress threatened not to give her a reference she enforced one with well informed and vitriolic threats. One she left after a fierce quarrel with the cook, and in another she poured boiling water over the arm and hand of the parlourmaid. In 1923 she lost all her money, which she had invested in cotton shares: she visited the office of the defaulting company and opened the face of the unhappy reception-clerk from mouth to eye with a blow from the ferrule of her umbrella. The magistrate reprimanded her severely but did not sentence her as it was her first offence and she had undoubtedly a real grievance. She was out of work for several weeks afterwards.

The sight of her Aunt Ethel made things worse for her: Ethel had sold her Cherry Hinton shop and gone into munitions too (she had been just young enough), but she had kept her money. She had bought houses with it in the Bloomsbury district, and had had sense enough to choose the West side of Gray's Inn

Road. Values had gone up, and now Ethel was comfortably off. She rigidly refused to lend Victoria a penny, but promised to remember her in her will, together with her younger sister, May Ena, and a waif named Irene Olga Hutchins, sole reminder of the two younger male Atkinses... "two" because there was a regrettable doubt which of them was the father, and both were beyond reach of questioners in a Flanders cemetery. Their last letters to the mother had been brief and unfriendly, consisting only of a refusal to pay, couched in identical terms. Irene now did practically all the housework for Great-Auntie, sustained by promises that in due course she would be a rich woman. The figures varied: sometimes it would be three thousand, sometimes five, and once even ten, that Irene was told she could expect as her third share when Great-Auntie passed on. Great-Auntie never spoke so detailedly to Victoria, of course, but Irene naturally told her disagreeable aunt whatever she chose to ask, and there were few things about which she asked more frequently.

So, in 1927, there were only four members of the once numerous Atkins family left, as far as was known, anyway. There were Aunt Ethel, Victoria herself, her sister May, and the small niece, whose unfortunate lack of the surname Atkins was forgotten, as she was invariably called nothing but Young Irene. Of these four, the last three were in indigent circumstances, and the first had plenty of money. This circumstance formed the first and most essential of the facts in a dossier assembled by the police in the winter of that year.

*

The next significant fact was an event that the police never noted in their records at all. On a Thursday afternoon in late November,

May, who spelt her name Mae even before Miss West wiped out any memory of Princess May, was taking tea with Victoria in Mrs. Mulholland's boarding-house in Lewisham. It was Victoria's custom to entertain her sister once a week, more to insist on her rights than from family affection, and also to provide for herself by fair exchange a place to go to on her own afternoon off.

Mae laid down her cup. "Tea's not up to much," she said, rather diffidently.

"And that's a fact," replied Victoria equably. "The old girl's mean. I don't know where she gets the tea; she brings it in herself. Mouse-dirt I found in it last time; *inside* the packet, mind you. I—Don't you feel well, Mae?"

"I do seem to have come over queer," said Mae faintly.

"Are you going to be *sick*?" said Victoria, with the anxious rising tone in which those words are always said.

"I'm afraid so…"

"Well, for goodness' sake run *quick*; you know where the W is," snapped her elder sister, shooing her out.

Mae was very sick indeed; her sister even relented and came to hold her head, so deplorable were the noises. Actually no harm resulted whatever; Mae's health was, if anything, improved by the upset, and you might have thought she had merely taken unintentionally a dose of ipecacuanha. But at the moment she felt she was going to die and miserably said so. Her sister was sympathetic, most unusually.

"I don't like it at all, Mae; I don't. You look as white as anything. Suppose there is something really wrong. You go straight home this moment and lie down. I'll come round and see you in, the morning, first thing I can. It's no good my asking the old cat for permission to go out to-night; but I'll get up early and the moment I've laid breakfast I'll pop across."

She fussed over her sister and bundled her out, very surprised and a little unwilling. But Mae was a little scared, too: Victoria had never shown anything like this sisterly anxiety. Perhaps she was really ill? Personally she'd have said it was nothing but Victoria's nasty tea, and the mention of mouse-dirt in it had been enough to turn any one up. Anyway she'd better go and if Victoria came round in the morning it couldn't do any harm.

Victoria watched her sister from the basement window with a curiously pleased expression. She said nothing to Mrs. Mulholland about the incident.

*

About five o'clock next morning the figure of a middle-sized woman in black with a veil could have been, but was not, seen moving at a sedate pace down a poorish street in Camberwell. Her feet made no sound; she presumably was wearing rubber-soled shoes. She went straight up to the corner house, which was Aunt Ethel's, and let herself in with a key, absolutely silently. There was a bolt on the inner side of the door, but the wood had warped years ago, and it could not be shot into its socket. The woman stood a full half-minute inside the door, listening. There was no sound at all except the ticking of a large hall-clock.

With a firm silent step, as of someone who knew her way, she moved across to Aunt Ethel's bedroom, turned the handle softly and listened. Steady breathing. The door closed behind her.

In the room there is darkness, except for the faint glimmer of the pillow case and turned down sheet: on the pillow a dim round marks the place where the old lady's head lies. A dark figure is standing beside the bed: you could not, if you were there, make out precisely what its hands are doing. They seem to be reaching underneath the old lady's head to her second pillow. To steal something? No, it is the second pillow itself the hands want. And, sudden speed contrasting with previous caution, the pillow is swept away and down on to the old lady's face; and there pressed down with fanatical energy. The sleeper breaks into violent and blind activity; her legs thrash madly about in the bed, her helpless, rather clawlike hands grab into the empty air but never find her attacker. The pillow drowns any sounds she may try to make.

These few minutes seem to last an hour. Down and down the hands press. The struggles grow weaker, but the hands cannot wait for them to end. The strong fingers separate the feathers in the pillow till they feel beneath them the skin of the throat. Then both thumbs with a sort of fierce delight thrust downwards and hold.

A little while later there is a slight sigh and the black figure straightens up. A spark of light appears, as from a small, nearly run out electric torch. By its light the pillow is removed and above the old lady's mouth appears, held in the air, a little mirror such as is carried in a vanity bag. No clouding on it, no moisture. The mirror is held there until its owner is satisfied it would remain clear for ever, and then the light is snapped out. In the dark, hands put back the pillow and roughly rearrange the bed; the black figure slips silently out again.

Back into the street. Two turnings, past silent homes and unwinking electric lights. Round into the main road and straight to a telephone box. The woman in black put in her twopence and dialled, not 999, but the local police station. When the answer came she said in an oddly high-pitched but not loud voice: "Oh, come at once, come at once! Me great-auntie's dead. Ow, it's too frightful... She's dead, I tell you, and I'm all alone. Are you going to leave me to be murdered?... It's 68 Duke Street... Oh, get *here* and don't ask silly questions." The station sergeant, who tried to stem and answer this rush of frightened words, automatically noted the time of the call before he turned to take action. It was 5.52 a.m.

The woman rang off, and then after a moment's hesitation rang Ethel's number. Ethel was rich and did have a telephone. She heard the ringing tone for quite a time, and then Irene's voice answered. "What do you want at this time of night?" it asked querulously. The woman in black made no reply: she pressed button B, took her twopence and went away. Irene would be up and awake now; she could let the police officers in and maybe do a little explaining to them. The woman in black walked away from the telephone box and in a minute or two took her place on an early workman's tram which was already in sight. Every one, including the conductor, was sleepy, and she was inconspicuous. She might be any rather superior charlady going to work. Nobody was likely to notice and remember her, and nobody did.

*

At exactly six o'clock, trained by years of experience, Mrs. Mulholland awoke temporarily, looked at her watch and listened to hear if the servant was getting up. Victoria had been late once or twice recently. She heard distantly the tinkle of the girl's alarum which was stopped almost immediately. Soon after there came the unmistakable bump of a chair being knocked over. "How clumsy that girl is getting," she thought, and turned over for another half-hour's sleep. Her cup of tea would come at 6.30.

6.40. No cup of tea. Mrs. Mulholland rose, wrapped a dressing-gown round herself, and called downstairs. "Victoria!" There was no answer. Cross and cold, she pattered down to the kitchen. Breakfast was laid, trays put out, curtains drawn, and everything tidy. But no kettle was on and in the middle of the table was a folded note:

> *Madam,—Having heard my sister Mae was very ill yesterday I have just slipped out to see how she is. Am sorry if this causes any inconvenience but I am very anxious and think I should know. Will be back as quickly as possible.*
>
> V. M. Atkins.

Mrs. Mulholland was very angry, and when Victoria returned well after seven, threatened her with dismissal. Victoria was unmoved—said it was just as Mrs. Mulholland pleased, that she had no father nor mother and it was her duty to look after her younger sister, and that she was glad to say, though not asked, that her sister was much better. Mrs. Mulholland considered the matter, remembered the rarity of good maids, and agreed to overlook it. Victoria went upstairs, tidied her bedroom, brought down and threw in the fire two scraps of string and a candle end, and nothing further happened of note until the police arrived later in the morning.

*

The police had had some difficulty in getting into 68 Duke Street. Irene had gone back to bed, and when induced to answer the door told them the message was nonsense. At last she consented to summon her great-aunt, and went into her room. A few seconds later she began to scream shrilly, and intermittently, rather like a steam engine. The two policemen—one in mufti—hurriedly shut the front door and ran into the bedroom. In a minute one of them came back again, went to the telephone and summoned the police doctor. There was no doubt the old lady was dead, and two very indistinct marks on the throat made it look like strangulation. The body was warm: it seemed only just dead. The time, the inspector noted, was 6.15.

For a short while it looked like an "open and shut" case. The young girl, Irene, was obviously prostrated by grief and shock. She was hardly strong enough to strangle the old lady, anyway, and if she was the murderer the mysterious telephone call was very difficult to explain. She insisted that she had never made it; that she had indeed been called up a quarter of an hour or so earlier to answer the telephone, but there was no one there by the time she got to it. Inspector Hodson acquitted her mentally: adding that apart from anything else no girl of her age could be so consummate an actress. Also she had told him that her Aunt Victoria was co-heir to the old lady's money and had a key to the door. He verified for himself that the bolt would not fit.

When the constable sent to break the news to Victoria came back with the report that she had left early that morning on an errand and returned late, he hastened across to Lewisham to conduct the inquiries himself. He was pretty certain the case was solved, especially as Irene had found time between tears to mention her aunt's very disagreeable temper.

*

What followed is perhaps best given by quoting certain questions and answers.

Q.—I hope you understand, Mrs. Mulholland, that I have to ask a few questions, mainly as a matter of form.

A.—If you get on with your job quickly, young man, it will let me get back the sooner to mine. I have to work for my living.

Q.—You employ a Miss Victoria Atkins as a servant?

A.—The constable's told you that already.

Q.—Well. Did she leave the house early this morning?

A.—Yes, she did. Left me to do all the hard work of the breakfasts, without permission or anything. I've agreed to overlook it, as she's a good servant; but it's not to occur again.

Q.—I don't suppose it will, ma'am. Now do you happen to be able to say just when she went out?

A.—Not to the minute, but it was some time after six.

Q.—After six? Are you sure? Much after six?

A.—I am sure. I'm not in the habit of speaking inaccurately. She got up at six, because I heard her alarm go and heard her get up, and a noise she made about it, too. No consideration for others' sleep. I expect Miss Meakin heard her, too: she has the other top room, which is cheap, Miss Meakin not having very much money but a very nice lady. Then Victoria went down and did the rooms and went out without saying a word to me, leaving this letter. I didn't hear her shut the door: she was sly enough to do it quietly. So I couldn't say just when she left. About twenty-past six, it must have been.

Q.—Yes. Thank you. I'll keep this letter if I may, for a bit. May I see your watch?

A.—See my watch? What for? Very well.

Q.—You haven't wound it up, or altered the hands, since this morning? Or let it out of your possession?

A.—Certainly not. What would I do that for?

Q.—Are you quite sure that Miss Atkins got up at the time you mentioned?

A.—I've said so.

Q.—How long did her alarm clock ring?

A.—The usual: a few seconds only.

Q.—What did you hear her do afterwards? Clean the grates and pull the curtains or what?

A.—Really, I can't say. I heard her get up and bang the furniture about, but I didn't notice exactly what. As a matter of fact, I took a little nap again afterwards, as is my habit, waiting for my tea. Anyway, I found everything tidy and all the work done downstairs, I'll say that. But that didn't mean I didn't have to make the tea myself and cook the breakfasts. And if you want any more information about what Victoria did you'd better ask her yourself.

(Note to above: Evidence from Miss Meakin confirms.)

*

More questions:

Q.—Your name, please.

A.—Mae Ena Atkins. What do you want?

Q.—Could you tell me what time your sister Victoria called on you this morning, and why?

A.—That's a funny thing to ask. I suppose it's all right. There's nothing wrong in it anyway. I was awful sick yesterday, and Vick said she'd come round early this morning to see if I was all right. Well, I don't blame her, seeing that she works for such an unpleasant old cat and has to take what times she can, but it was a little inconsiderate to come round as early as all that. You see, I'd told my lady, a very nice lady, that I'd been taken queer, and she'd said I could have a bit of a rest and so I was having a nice lay-in for once and then Vick has to come round in an awful fuss at twenty to seven and get everybody up, just to see if I was all right.

Q.—Twenty to seven! Surely she didn't do that.

A.—Oh, yes, she did. I said to her "I do appreciate it," I said, "and I'd have you know that I do; but it really isn't sensible to wake every one up at this time in the morning, Vicky," and she said "It's seven and more," and I said "It's nothing of the sort"; but she wouldn't have it until I made her look at the clock on St. Michaels, and there it was as clear as you please. And then she was a bit huffy, and went back after no more than a few words.

Q.—Mm—mm. Is it far from here to where your sister works?

A.—About twenty minutes on a bus. I've often done it.

Q.—You spent the night here, I suppose, in the usual way?

A.—Why, of course, I did. I told you I was not at all well; why should I run about the streets at night anyway? Madam very kindly gave me a glass of hot milk and three aspirins; I went straight off to sleep and never moved till I was woken up by Vick.

(There is no need to transcribe the notes of the examination of Mae's employer. The essential sentences were:

"I told Mae she was to go to bed early as she had been sick, and make herself a glass of hot milk. I went upstairs and saw she was in bed by half-past nine and made her take three aspirins. I gave them her myself; and told her I would get my hubby's breakfast for once myself. So far as I know she slept right through until we were all woken up by that disagreeable sister of hers.")

*

Q.—Your name is Victoria Atkins?

A.—Yes.

Q.—I believe you've heard that your aunt has died suddenly. We are making a few inquiries, and I hope you won't mind answering a few questions.

(No answer.)

Q.—When did you last see your aunt?

A.—Last week. I forget which day. Irene would tell you. She looked quite well.

Q.—You didn't see her this morning?

A.—No.

Q.—What did you do this morning?

A.—I got up at the usual time—six o'clock—tidied up downstairs, and left a note for the missus. I ran out to see my sister Mae, who hadn't been at all well. I found she was better, and came back straight here. That's all. Why are you asking me these questions?

Q.—Was your aunt well-to-do?

A.—I couldn't say. She wasn't hard-up that I know of.

Q.—I suppose she will have left you something in her will?

A.—It's not the sort of thing I care to discuss with the poor lady not yet cold in her grave.

Q.—Still—

A.—In well-bred circles that is all that needs to be said. I would have you remember that I've had a very severe shock and while I will answer any reasonable questions I'm not going to listen to idle chitchat. Aunt Ethel will have done whatever she thought right and that is all any one is entitled to know.

Q.—Oh, yes, of course, of course. Now let me see if I've got everything right: You got up—about when? Some time before six, was it?

A.—Six exactly. And down in about ten minutes.

Q.—Yes, yes. And then you tidied up and laid the table. Pulled the curtains, I suppose?

A.—I don't remember any details: I was worrying about my sister. I got to her as soon as I could—a little earlier than I meant to. Just before seven, I think.

*

There were many other questions and answers, but they got the police no further. The constable whose beat went past Mrs. Mulholland's house had noticed during the night that the sitting-room curtains were not drawn as usual. But this information seemed to lead nowhere. Elaborate questioning failed to find any one who had noticed a suspicious character, or any character, in Duke Street that morning. The dial system prevented tracing the telephone call.

Irene came for a while under suspicion, but it was found that she had a half withered arm and physically could never have committed the crime. Inspector Hodson himself was convinced that Victoria was guilty, but her defence seemed impregnable. Both her mistress and Miss Meakin remembered clearly hearing her get up, and though they were not certain as to when she left, there was no reasonable doubt that it was after six, when two policemen were standing by Ethel's newly-dead-body, a good half-hour away.

In the end Victoria inherited £2,327 11s. od. from her aunt and purchased with it a tobacconist's and newsagent's business. In three years' time she had made enough to buy her house; and this new prosperity was responsible for her receiving a juror's summons. She spent 7s. 6d. with a lawyer, to receive the information that she could not escape her duties; and in consequence, half displeased, half interested, she made her way to court on the day.

She thought to herself, in a manner as near to humour as any thought of hers could be, that it wouldn't half be queer if she had to be juror in a murder case. Somebody who did know how judging somebody that didn't. For she never attempted to forget that she had killed her aunt, and she never had the least regret. She was rather proud of it, though she remembered having several bad scares and was certain she'd never do such a thing again.

It had been pretty simple. The alarum clock was easy. Even the coppers had suspected that. It was only a matter of testing the winding, and she'd done that several times, holding the bell in her handkerchief. She had found exactly the number of turns of the alarum key necessary to make it ring twenty seconds and no more. Then she had set it and left it. She had been intentionally irregular in her getting up for some days before, to make sure Mrs. Mulholland would listen for her alarum. Anyway, Miss Meakin was safe. There is sometimes a very slight difference between an alarum that has run down and one that is cut short, but it is not the sort of thing a sleepy woman notices, let alone remembers to tell a rozzer.

The bumping of the furniture had been a little more difficult. But only a little patience was needed, and sleeping with your window shut to avoid a draught. Candles burn exactly to time: didn't the Romans use them as clocks or something? Victoria had spent many nights testing and re-testing their speed, marking out the hours, halves, and quarters on them. She didn't use her knowledge until she was absolutely certain to a few minutes either way. Then on the night she pulled her blind down and arranged what looked like a sort of booby trap.

To a nail driven into the window-sill she attached a long piece of string; the other end she tied to the wooden chair which was almost her complete bedroom furniture. She leant the chair against her bed, tipped to one side. If the string were to break, it would fall down to the floor on its side, with a reasonable but not excessive noise.

Then she made a triangular cut in the candle on the table by her bed, at a particular place which she had marked. She moved the table underneath the string, so that the string pressed into the triangular cut, right against the wick, and then, taking the time from her watch, lit the candle. Unless her calculations were wrong, the candle flame would reach the place at six exactly, and in a minute or so the string would snap.

Her calculations were not wrong; on top of that she had a bit of luck on which she had not reckoned. People hear what they expect to hear. Miss Meakin and Mrs. Mulholland had for day after day heard Victoria's alarum go off, then heard her bump about a bit while dressing, and after that if they strained their ears heard her move faintly and distantly doing the kitchen out downstairs. When, half asleep, they heard the beginning of this process they assumed that they had heard the rest. If Inspector Hodson had cross-questioned both of them closely and immediately that very morning he might perhaps have raised a doubt in their minds whether Victoria's getting up was actually followed by the usual sounds of work downstairs. Even if he had, as the inspector knew very well, doubt about almost any evidence can be induced by sufficiently long cross-examination: results obtained that way don't generally stand up too well in court. Anyway, when he did examine the two ladies in detail, they showed none of the phenomenal feats of detailed memory that occur in detective stories. They merely remembered that things had gone as usual that morning, and said so.

It had taken a bit of nerve (Victoria remembered) to go on to Mae's after It, instead of hurrying back. But as soon as she got home she had gone back upstairs, pulled up the blind, made the bed, set the chair straight, wound up the alarum, and twisted the nail out. She'd put in a new candle and let it burn a minute. She'd taken the two ends of string and the candle stump and thrown them on the kitchen fire. So even if the coppers had gone over her room they must have found nothing.

She was day-dreaming to this effect, standing with the other jurors, when the clerk caught her attention.

"I swear by Almighty God," she repeated after him, "that I will well and truly try, and true deliverance make between our Sovereign Lord the King and the prisoner at the bar whom I shall have in charge, and a true verdict give according to the evidence." Silly way of talking, she thought; kissed the book and sat down on the bench for the jurors already sworn.

2

The Clerk of Assize turned next to the man whom he had noticed as being unusually handsome. Like most men of past middle-age he habitually faintly disliked or distrusted handsome men, especially dark handsome men. If there was any excuse he would classify them as shiny or foreign looking. A man was all the better for being a bit rugged looking, and all the worse for having regular features and being noticeably well-groomed. However, even he had nothing against this juror. After a quite perceptible stare he said to him: "Arthur George Popesgrove, repeat after me..."

ARTHUR GEORGE POPESGROVE. A VERY ENGLISH NAME. ONLY an Englishman or an American could say Arthur correctly; George was the King's name; and no one would think that Popesgrove had been taken out of the telephone directory. Sometimes the owner of the name wished he had selected Anthony as first name. Though he was rather darker, his face had a distinct resemblance to the Rt. Hon. Anthony Eden's, and it was no fault of his if his clothes were not identically the same. Certainly, Mr. Eden could never have been more conscious than he was of being English. No other member of the jury felt that to be called to serve was a high privilege: at the best they accepted it as a duty. Arthur Popesgrove was delighted when he opened the summons. "You see, Maud," he said to his wife, "I have to be a juror now. That is very important. I take my part in safeguarding British justice." He smiled contentedly—his wife looked down her nose and said nothing. Her nose was fat, large and white; very wide at the base and with blackheads; it was not a very English nose. But after all you could not order your wife to change her nose. At least she answered to the name Maud without protest, and they never spoke anything but English in the home. English; he was wholly English, for his naturalization papers were the evidence of will and choice, whereas the birth certificate of the man next door was only evidence of an accident. None of his children should ever know that their blood was anything but English. If necessary, even the cooking in his restaurant should change. Already he had one man parading the grillroom floor behind a great silver dish on which was a huge roast sirloin. When patrons asked for his advice he very often would say: "After all, there's nothing like really good roast beef, is there, sir? Or a steak, perhaps? Scorched outside and red inside." Stuffed vine-leaves had disappeared from the list: garlicky dishes were less common.

The size of his family was perhaps a little un-English. He had had six children before observing that large families were unfashionable as well as uneconomic. Their names however were unimpeachable. Eric Archibald, Julia, James Henry, Mary, Charles Edward, and Arthur Herbert. Try and mess about with *those*. His own accent was impeccable. Once he used to hiss his esses slightly, but there was no trace of that now. He had even prepared, in case of need, a false genealogy for his children. He would tell them that their mother came from the Channel Islands, and that their grandfather, on his side, had been a bit of a rogue. "We don't talk about him, but it's your right to know," he saw himself saying. "He was the son of a small Dorset landowner who came up to town and spent his money wildly. He got into a fight one night and a policeman died as a result. He had a rather heavy sentence. I don't remember him; I was only a kid then."

He felt certain that he was doing his children a far more real service by telling them this story than by disclosing the truth. Yet few people but himself would have felt that there was anything shameful in the origin of A. G. Popesgrove, restaurant proprietor. It went back to a Thessalian village—dry, poverty stricken, smelly and under a brilliant sun which never shines in England, even on the brightest summer day. The sun is never an enemy here: it does not burn your skin with its heat, and spike your eyes with its brightness. The blue sky is never hateful and metallic. The countryside is rarely brown and burnt, with clouds of dust rising and blowing all over your food and clothes. The smells may not be better, but they are different and they are not eternal and unvarying.

The little boy, Achilles Papanastasiou, handsome as only a Greek small boy can be, very early decided that the best thing that he could do was to get away from this village as soon as he could. He did not mind how he did it; and a quarter of a century later he truly did not remember how he had done it. But the way was this.

Greek politics before the war were a little more open than they are to-day, but they did not differ in essence. Colonel Theseus Theotoki was a politician, and on one of his election tours he noticed young Achilles. He went to his parents and bought him, as he might have bought a calf. There was a little more palaver about it: he spoke of Athens, of a liberal education, and of the opportunities which the secretary of a political leader would have, and the transaction was registered at the town hall as an adoption.

Young Achilles immediately found out that his duties included more intimate services than secretarial work. The colonel owned certain private houses and hotels which were run in direct contravention of the law. That was not very serious, but a certain discretion had nevertheless to be observed. Quiet semi-blackmail was possible. By the time Achilles was sixteen he realized he had a lever which he could use against the colonel. So for a short time Achilles had a great deal of money. Athens was very gay: the war was on and there was plenty of amusement of a normal kind, which was what Achilles preferred. The colonel seemed an inexhaustible resource, and Achilles went out on a permanent binge.

So far it did not matter. But Achilles was very inexperienced; he was, after all, only a raw boy from a village. He committed the enormous imprudence of becoming arrogant as well as wasteful. He spent his patron's money mercilessly and failed to perform any of the duties for which he was paid. The gambling rooms and the rooms where other pleasures were provided did not see him for nights on end. He was supposed to act as a sort of male "hostess," as an encourager of extravagance, as assistant chucker-out and occasionally pickpocket. He didn't. Colonel Theseus protested for a while, and then suddenly realized he was being made a fool of. He remembered he possessed a certain influence still, and went to see the chief of police.

Achilles was drinking in a wine shop in the Peiraieus that afternoon. He had not had very much to drink yet, he was quiet and sober, and slightly uneasy about his patron's manner that morning. He was more than a little disquieted when the girl serving in the saloon, who was about a year younger than him, said to him in a low, clear whisper:

"Get out. Leave Athens this afternoon and don't go back home. I'm warning you."

She left him gaping and went back to her work. After a minute he signed to her.

"A glass of uzo. What did you mean by what you said just now?"

His hand roamed round her behind.

"Stop that, silly. This is serious. Two policemen" (she used an exceedingly offensive Greek word which had no English equivalent) "were here an hour ago. They talked about you. I knew it was you because they mentioned Colonel Theotoki. This evening you'll be arrested. A sailor will charge you with [an indecent offence]. You'll be proved to have assaulted the police as well. You'll get prison, and deportation to one of the islands, they think."

"You made it up."

"I didn't. You wait and see. If you go back to the colonel's place they've got something else. I didn't understand exactly what, but it was something to do with stealing."

Achilles turned rather green, and felt sick. He had been a little free with the colonel's jewellery. What did an old man want with bracelets, anyway?

"What's your name?" he said.

"Helena Melagloss. Are you going?"

He sat for a few minutes silent and then went down to the port. There were plenty of jobs on Allied transports for able bodied youngsters, and no questions asked.

*

Right until the end of the war he worked on French boats, usually in the galley, as a sort of pantry boy. He was well fed, learnt

French thoroughly, and certain rudiments of cooking. He also learnt to be quick with a knife. He caught a disease and was cured of it summarily by the ship's surgeon, who scared him into a cautious method of life by a highly exaggerated medical lecture. He deserted from his ship on November 18th, 1918, at Marseilles, with no passport or other papers at all, except a seaman's card showing he had served on French transports for two years.

His money lasted very few days, and he was rescued half-starving in Toulon by a compatriot whose real name remained for ever unknown to him. No one ever called him anything but Monsieur Dimo. Monsieur Dimo owned a small hotel-restaurant in the harbour district. The restaurant trade was cheap but decent. The trade in hotel rooms was almost wholly for prostitutes; Achilles was kept continuously making and re-making the same beds every night. His duties went on regularly until one and two in the morning, and sometimes later. They restarted at 9 o'clock. He had to clean out the restaurant and tidy it, and then go into the kitchen, peel potatoes and do all a kitchen-maid's work. After that he must return to the restaurant and serve aperitifs. Then he must act as waiter until about three, when he would do the washing-up which had been too much for Madame Dimo. After that he was supposed to have some time to himself, but it was almost invariably taken from him on the grounds that it had been impossible for Madame to clean out the bedrooms in the morning. By half-past five preparations must begin for the evening dinners, and from then on work was continuous. He received no wages, only tips, and these he was supposed to share equally with Monsieur Dimo, though he soon learnt to cheat on that. Monsieur Dimo provided him with a passport and a *permis de séjour*, made out in the name of Anton Polycrate. He never knew whether there was any such person: on the whole, it is more probable that the passport was forged than stolen.

One day he decided that he could better himself by going along the coast to St. Raphael or Nice. He politely gave Monsieur Dimo notice. Monsieur Dimo narrowed his eyes.

"So you are going, my little one. I wonder. Perhaps I can persuade you to stay. I think I can."

Achilles smiled. A rise in wages—or, rather, wages at all—would do as well.

"The French police," reflected Monsieur Dimo, "are very severe on aliens who creep in on false passports. A term in the *cachot* and then deportation: that is the very least. I have a suspicion that your papers that you carry are not your own. I think the *gendarmes* would like to know what happened to its real owner.

"I would advise you to stay with me. If you run away, and I tell the police to look for you, they will find you very soon."

Achilles remained silent for a moment. Then he said:

"I shall expect a very good reference from you, Monsieur Dimo."

Monsieur Dimo replied very quietly with a single very rude word.

"I think you will give it me, Monsieur Dimo. I am far from wishing to avoid the police. Indeed, there are many things on which I would like their advice. I shall tell them that I am an honest Greek boy; I can speak but cannot read French. I can only read the Greek alphabet, you see. I have a piece of paper which I know shows that I served France loyally through great dangers throughout two whole years of war. But these papers," he looked

doubtfully at his passport and *permis* "were obtained for me by
kind Monsieur Dimo, who said that he would perform all formali-
ties. I do not understand them. But I will have to tell the Chief of
Police that I am worried because Monsieur Dimo seems to have so
many of these papers to give people. So many of my unfortunate
countrymen are obliged by him that I am wondering if my papers
are all right. The policeman at the corner is very sympathetic; I
shall ask him if I ought to speak to the chief also about Monsieur
Dimo's hotel. I am troubled, especially about that pretty girl who
was injured by the American."

He looked sadly up at the ceiling.

Monsieur Dimo gave an unamused smile. "I think we will
talk about this this evening," he said, "if you really insist on this
foolishness."

Achilles was not waiting till nightfall. Disagreeable things
happen at night. "I am going now," he said. "Either I go towards
the Riviera with your recommendation and 100 francs for wages.
Or I go with these papers to the police."

He looked magnificently calm, but he was not in the least comfortable. Fortunately, Monsieur Dimo was still less comfortable.

"Very well," he said angrily. "You wait here while I get the
money."

"No," said Achilles. "I wait outside, where I can see the *gen-
darme*. And you bring it to me."

★

A young Levantine who was willing to work, was a promising
cook, was a graceful and even beautiful waiter and dancer, and
had few scruples or inhibitions. The Riviera in 1920. Take these
factors together and you will see it was impossible not to make

money. Polycrate—he adopted this name for a while—made it; moreover, he saved it. As he estimated the guests of all nations who passed through the big hotels where he served, he decided that only English and Americans had real money. He changed his savings into dollars. Whenever he could, he gave English speakers especially good service: in his mind was springing up a hope that he might be invited to a post in New York or London. Chef to a duke or a millionaire: that would be an ideal job.

He never got it, but he did get to London. If we say that he got to London as a result of his special attentions to an English hotel proprietor, we should tell the truth while conveying a lie. Things did not fit in so neatly with abstract justice.

Mr. Bernard Hubbard was not a discerning epicure, nor Achilles a startlingly good cook. Mr. Hubbard had bought a controlling share in Imperial and Universal Hotels, Ltd., and was determined to show what a Lancashire business man could do with an organization like that. There were hundreds of Mr. Hubbards about while the cotton boom lasted: few of them had anything to them but brass in both senses of the word. Bernard Hubbard was obstinate and arrogant; he had plenty of money which did not stay with him very long; he knew nothing whatever about cooking and hotel service, though he did know a certain amount about organization. He had come to the Riviera to get a number of first-class chefs. He would not take advice—he would ask for it, and then cunningly refuse to act upon it, in case wool was being pulled over his eyes. He was a good judge of faggots, black pudding and fish and chips, but the French menus he could not even read. Immobilized by his ignorance and his suspicions, he had hired nobody at all after a whole month in Nice and Cannes.

He had dined once before at the hotel where Achilles was working as head waiter. He came in one afternoon and reserved himself a table for two—he was to entertain a blonde who has no especial part in this story. "And mind the food's better to-night than it was last time. It was thoroughly second-rate. I expect something special." He complained merely on general principles.

"I will see to it myself, sir," said Achilles, bowing, and forgot the whole matter at once.

When he saw Mr. Hubbard arrive with his blonde he came forward with a glad recognition which suggested that nothing else but the forthcoming dinner had been in his mind all the evening. As he bowed them to their table he was thinking fast. The menu was neither good nor bad, but there was nothing that even Mr. Hubbard could be deluded into thinking special. *Gigot de pré salé. Escalope de veau. Blanquette de veau. Boeuf à la mode. Poulet rôti. Perdreau en casserole.* It was all pretty unimaginative. The partridge was perhaps the best bet. He recommended to Mr. Hubbard caviare, cold soup (both of which the Lancashire man disliked but ordered to impress the blonde), sole *meunière*.

"And then, sir, there is the special dish for you. A partridge cooked in a special way. It is not on the menu."

Mr. Hubbard, as in duty bound, made a sceptical noise, but accepted the partridge. Achilles went back to the kitchen, placed the rest of the order and considered the partridge. "Can you fix the partridge en casserole to make it look a little different?" he asked the chief chef. "There's an Englishman out there who insists on something special."

The chef looked at him morosely. Waiters were thieves who took all the tips and did no serious work. They were a sort of gigolo who deserved the contempt of any honest artisan.

"You can't do anything else with these partridges," he said. "They are frozen anyway and have not been hung long enough. Unless you do them en casserole they will be too tough to eat."

"A more tasty sauce, perhaps—" began Achilles.

"The sauce is naturally," replied the cook, "wholly perfect. All that can be done with such indifferent material has been done. Since the birds have no taste, that is perceived. It cannot be prevented. When I am given filth to cook with, besides having my time wasted by chatter, what do you expect? The birds are cooked in wine, with mushrooms, onions, and herbs. They are a beautiful brown to look at. They are good enough for the English, anyway. Too good."

Achilles tasted one of the birds which was ready to serve. It was true; it had very little taste. The sauce was competently made, as it was being made in a hundred other restaurants at that minute. He returned to his duties disconsolately.

After he had served Mr. Hubbard the fish he came back into the kitchen. Zero hour: he must do something. His eye lighted on an orange. Oranges were served with duck: very well, then. He sliced it quickly and handed it to the chef.

"Chuck that into the casserole for No. 5, and leave it in the oven for five minutes."

Shortly afterwards he was serving with a flourish a golden brown bird surrounded by bright golden rings. As he took the dish away he tasted the remains of the sauce. All was well: there was a pleasant tang in it which had saved the whole thing from insipidity.

Mr. Hubbard was saying: "This ought to be something special, my dear."

"Ow," said blonde. "I fought vey only served oranges wiv duck."

Whether it was suggestion, or that he really did perceive the excellence of the flavour, Mr. Hubbard was pleased. When Achilles returned to ask if everything was satisfactory, he beamed.

"Where d'you get the idea of shoving the oranges in? Ought only to do that with duck, you know."

"That is an essential part of the cooking, monsieur. Part of the new idea."

"The new idea? You can't come that, my boy. Are you trying to tell me you made that up? Oh, no, no."

"That is just so, monsieur. I have been considering the question during the afternoon. A partridge has never been cooked this way before. I invented it. I supervised it myself. Monsieur may ask the chef himself, if he so pleases."

Mr. Hubbard gazed at him with what he believed was a shrewd expression.

"Hum!" he said. "Well, it was good. What is your name?"

"Anton Polycrate, monsieur."

Next morning Anton Polycrate accepted, after a little decorous resistance, a contract with Imperial and Universal Hotels at £750 a year for three years, and 2,500 francs to placate the restaurant management for breaking his contract with them. He had no contract, but as they never heard of the 2,500 francs, that was all right. Mr. Hubbard charged himself with all questions of securing visas and labour permits.

★

It was from that day that his life—his real life—began. He realized when he landed in London that he was in a new world, and
a new life would have to be constructed. All that he had been
and all that he had done was gone over, tested, and for the most
part thrown away and forgotten. There was, however, one great
exception. A solid citizen, Greek or English, needs one thing at
least to establish his solidity. When he had been two months in
London he went to his bank manager, who treated him with the
respect due to a customer who had a comfortable small balance
and had been introduced with a warm letter from the Société
Générale. Did they have a branch in Athens? They did. Could they
arrange—at a proper fee, of course—for the transfer of a small
sum of money to a friend who might have changed her address?
They could make inquiries, and would do their best.

He reflected for some days, and then with a sudden abandon
instructed the bank to advance to Helena Melagloss, employed in
1916 in the Café Demosthenes in the Peiraieus, the price of a single
fare to London and a passport fee, provided that she appeared
before their local manager and swore that she was not married
nor the mother of any children. To the art editor of *Eleftheron
Bema*, whom he had known slightly he sent £25, asking him to
keep £5 for himself as a sort of search fee, and to find out the
present position of Miss Melagloss. The letter was couched in
an extravagant and rhetorical tone of friendship—a style which
even as he wrote he promised himself never to use again—but
its essential instructions were absolutely clear. The editor was to
assure himself that Helena was not married, not a mother, not on
the streets and in good health. When he was satisfied on all these
four points he was to ask her what she had called the policemen

acting for Colonel Theotoki, and to hand her a letter and £20. The letter contained a proposal of marriage, and instructions to go to the bank.

The editor kept £20 and gave Helena £5 and the letter. He made no inquiries at all (except about the word for policemen). Nor did Helena. She hardly remembered Achilles and she refused to say what she had called the policemen; but he seemed to have money, and anything was better than the life of a waitress in sea-men's cafés in Greece. She went to the unheard-of expense of telegraphing her acceptance, took ship and landed in London with the set intention of making a good and loyal wife to this young man, whoever he might be.

So soon as she grasped his intentions, she was even more single-minded in pursuing them. She it was who suggested the change of surname and Christian names by deed poll. She it was who insisted on those unending-seeming night-classes, at which they learned to say *th* correctly and even to spell reasonably well. She made Achilles, now Arthur, take the first steps for naturaliza-tion; she took the drastic step of banning all Greek in the home after the eldest child was two, even at the most intimate moments. "ζωὴ μοῦ, ψύχη μοῦ," Arthur said one evening, romantically and rashly remembering a scrap of classical education. She locked him out of the bedroom, and would not let him in until he had called through the door: "Oh, come on, Maud; be a sport."

And now she watched him reading the long official document, pleasure all over his face. If any questions or doubts ran through her head they left no trace on her face. "Do you think you will be foreman, Arthur?" she said admiringly, after a long pause.

"Hardly that, I should say."

"I don't see why not."

She was right: his confident manner and well-to-do appearance secured him the selection. Perhaps it was something, too, to do with the proud, almost regal tone in which he repeated the oath:

> "I swear by Almighty God that I will well and truly try, and true deliverance make between our Sovereign Lord the King and the prisoner at the bar whom I shall have in charge, and a true verdict give according to the evidence."

Splendid words, each phrase with a patina of history upon it. The consciousness of their meaning and their beauty seemed to radiate from him. No one could doubt, watching him, that he would indeed true deliverance make, as far as ever his powers would let him.

3

The Clerk of Assizes passed Mr. Popesgrove through, with a slight wave of his hand as if he had been in charge of a turnstile at the zoo. Glancing carelessly at the paper in his hand (for his mind was on the faces of the jurors waiting to be sworn) he said, "James Alfred Stannard..." and a short white-haired man moved forward out of his turn. "I beg your pardon," said the Clerk vexedly, "I should have said Percival Holmes, repeat after me..." The man at the end of the row moved forward to receive the Bible.

A YEAR BEFORE THIS TRIAL A YOUNG RHODES SCHOLAR HAD prevailed upon a friend to introduce him to the well-known Greek scholar and fellow of his college, Dr. Percival Holmes. Dr. Holmes (said the friend) was hardly ever in Oxford, and it was necessary to come to London to find him. Nor would it be possible to secure an appointment; but that did not mean the meeting need be left to chance. Dr. Holmes always lunched at one chosen place, and after lunch was accessible.

Somewhat to his surprise, the Rhodes scholar was piloted by his friend to a shabby dairy which had also a small teashop business. It was in a side-street, and looked doubtfully clean. Its white paint had become grey with age and in places had been scrubbed off showing green below. Inside there was a marble counter with a large milk bowl on it, a price list, three cakes with coconut on top and one with pink icing. The woman behind was middle-aged, dark, with glasses and in a white uniform.

"The professor here?" said the Rhodes' scholar's friend.

The woman jerked her head towards the brown partition, with frosted glass panes at the top, which cut off the end of the shop. She did not speak.

The two men walked through the partition door. Here the Rhodes scholar saw a sight which shocked his sense of fitness inexpressibly. There were six marble-topped tables in the dingy small room. Only one was occupied, as it was now a quarter to three; it, like all the rest, was dirty with crumbs, splashes of tomato sauce, and brown rings of saucer marks. On it were two black bottles and some thick tumblers, of the kind that are found in boarding house bedrooms. Behind it sat an enormously fat man in a grubby brown suit. He suggested a mass of cooking fat which had been poured into some sort of container and there congealed. It was difficult to conceive of him moving; and indeed he was utterly motionless except for his white fingers which trembled continuously. His pale blue eyes stared straight ahead; they were severely bloodshot and watering. A heavy smell of alcohol rose from him, together with another smell which might merely have been that of none-too-clean clothes, but which to the Rhodes scholar seemed a smell of death. The lower part of his body was concealed by the table; what could be seen appeared to be a perfect cone. The rather narrow-topped head was supported on thick greyish hanging rolls of fat which covered whatever neck there had once been; there were sloping shoulders and a vast paunch below.

"'Morning, Dr. Holmes," said the friend, "introduce Mr. Allinson, of your college. A Rhodes scholar."

"Ah!" said the gross figure, in a harsh and loud voice. "Port or moselle?"

The Rhodes scholar was perplexed and silent.

"Port or moselle?" shouted the doctor again, pushing forward the two bottles, which must have been his own property, as the shop had no licence. "Never drink anything else," he added, though it was not clear whether this was a command or a statement of his own habits.

"I'm not sure," began the American. "Port, I think," he added hastily, seeing anger rising in the doctor's face.

"Don't you *know*?" sneered the doctor. He poured nearly a half-pint of purple liquid into one of the tooth-glasses and pushed it across. The American drank a mouthful: it had that revolting taste of sugar, ink, and red pepper that only bad port can achieve.

Dr. Holmes meanwhile addressed his conversation to the friend, asking him about some college gossip which the American could not follow. It appeared to be scabrous, but that might merely have been the quality of Dr. Holmes's laugh, which was a sort of thick titter. Twice the American tried to intervene. The first effort was a carefully prepared question about Verrall's re-interpretation of the *Agamemnon*.

"Doctor" (he said "Dahcter," and Holmes made no attempt to conceal a shudder) "do you consider the Watchman's opening speech is to be read as an intentionally untruthful statement?"

"See chapter four of my *Essays on Greek Tragedy*," was the sole answer.

A little later he tried again.

"There are one or two points I'd be glad of your opinion on," he said.

"Don't you like your port?" replied the doctor, staring at the still half-full glass. The American, with the excessive courtesy which his nation so often shows to the elderly, learned and ill-mannered, took a fresh huge gulp of the disagreeable liquid. Tears came to his eyes and he had to fight back a feeling of sickness; meanwhile the doctor resumed his conversation with his friend.

The Rhodes scholar stood it for a few minutes more and then rose to go.

"You seem very busy," he said with restraint.

"Ah. Yes. Good-bye," said the doctor, swivelling his fat grey cheeks round to him for a moment, and then at once resuming his conversation.

Such were the manners and appearance of Dr. Percival Holmes at the age of 69, in every way the greatest contrast to those of Mr. James Alfred Stannard at 70. For Mr. Stannard was short, spare and neat, with a red face, white moustache, and thin white hair. He was moreover clean, and consistently polite to any one who was not drunk. Yet both men would have assumed that Dr. Holmes was a superior being. For he, though ill-bred, repulsive to look at, and grotesquely idle, was a gentleman; Mr. Stannard, who had worked hard all his life, who was kindly to all, and who was as agreeable in presence as he was in mind, kept a public-house. It was called the Hanging Gate.

The contrast so frequently drawn between the country inn and the London gin palace is the product of ignorance. Most of the London pubs are as much "locals" as any rural beerhouse. Mr. Stannard knew three-quarters of his clients every night, and knew, too, most of their sorrows and failings. The rough side of his tongue was kept exclusively for strange patrons who had taken too much drink. His normal gentleness wholly disappeared and he would snap: "No more for you, sir! And be so good as to leave this house immediately." His white moustache seemed to bristle and Fred, his son-in-law and chucker-out, would sidle near. Generally assistance was not required; Mr. Stannard's eye sufficed, supported by public opinion:

"That's ri'."

"I'd go off home, chum; I would."

"Had enough, I reckon."

His manner to friends who wished to exceed was quite different. He would fail to hear the order for a long time, and when it became impossible to continue, would fold his arms on the bar and lean over and conduct a slow conversation, consisting chiefly of the following sentences, arranged and rearranged in various orders:

"Now, do you really want to drink any more?"

"I'd have said you had rather a good deal, Bert."

"You know I have to think of my licence. I've been worried a great deal recently."

"Excuse me while I attend to that gentleman in the Private."

"You gentlemen, you tell me: Do you really think Bert wants any more?"

"Now you see, Bert, I don't feel I really could serve you after that."

Or alternatively, if the appeal to the audience was not answered rightly:

"I'm most surprised at you encouraging him. I'm not sure that I'm wise to serve any of you." A threat which generally produced a sudden silence and an exhortation to Bert to give over.

It was thirty years since his wife had died and his main interest was the life of the pub. Old friends came to see him every night: they told him of births, deaths, marriages, and trouble with the police or landlord. They waited for him to seal the subject with:

"Well, that's very nice; I'm sure they'll be very happy," or "Troubles never come singly." Each time the remark seemed charged with renewed meaning and importance. Life for him was a blurred series of warm golden evenings, blue fog of tobacco smoke, the sharp and sweet heavy smell of beer, the dart board full in his view, the steady roar of conversation. No day was separated from another in his memory. He took no holiday. For a week in August he sent away his daughter Gwen, the barmaid, and her husband to Margate, and with a considerable effort looked after the pub singlehanded. His one worry was the law, which is complicated enough for publicans, and was made worse for him by a nervousness dating from a trivial conviction for poaching in his extreme youth. On the only occasion when his licence was challenged he exhibited every sign of guilt. He turned alternately red and white, and stammered and could not answer the simplest question. He might very well have lost his licence if the police inspector in attendance had not intervened and effectively taken the conduct of the case away from him. He had declared that the Hanging Gate was in the police opinion the best conducted public-house in the district, and Mr. Stannard a most conscientious and careful licensee. He very nearly accused the Vicar of St. Barnabas' in so many words of evil-speaking and bearing false witness. (He saw himself a Baptist and the vicar was High Church.)

When Mr. Stannard received his juror's notice he was deeply distressed. A quite unreasoning terror overcame him and he remained seated in his corner in silent dejection for three nights on end. His digestion went entirely wrong; he drank nothing but weak gin and peppermint, and he refused all conversation. One evening he left the bar wholly to Fred and Gwen, and sat alone in the little back sitting-room over the fire, brooding. Policemen and law-courts: they meant no good and he was sure to make a fool of himself. He stared sullenly at the horsehair sofa and framed photograph of his wife above it, and gradually memories came back into his mind and soothed him. Dolly had died just before the war. End of 1913. Two months after his son Jim had gone to Australia, and Gwen only a little girl. He thought of his son, whom he had never seen since. A good boy, and doing well. Jim had three sons, whose photographs, with his daughter-in-law's, were on his mantelpiece. Each year Jim wrote to him on his birthday, and every Christmas he wrote back, short, difficult letters, with each letter slowly outlined in deep-pressed pencil, and ending *"your affect father, J. Stannard."* There was rarely anything in them but news of the family's health and the state of trade. World history was, as it were, seen through the bottom of a beermug. 1916 received this description:

"it is getting more difficult to obtain good beer and Twice recently I have run out of stout. Understand that owing to things in General we may be really short and have to refuse custom."

1917 was the year in which "I hardly See any of our old Regulars, and some will not be coming Back, am sorry to hear. The Place is full of women drinking as much as men, and would drink anything, but it's not what you like but what you can get the prices you would not Beleive."

1918: "The War being over every one was very merry and Drank Plenty, or would have: I was compelled to Open at eleven and soon was drunk out, and I believe every House round here the same."

Just about forty years he'd been in the house, he reflected. And a quarter of a century now without Dolly. Her memory was even a little dim; his thoughts slipped back to his childhood and young manhood in Suffolk, which for some reason stood out with greater clarity. Tall hedges and deeply rutted lanes. Walberswick Church, which to his memory was a gigantic ruin, a cathedral, in which one corner still standing was roofed over and used as a church by the few remaining worshippers. And especially horses: the horses belonging to the great house, where he was employed. No motor-cars then. He tried to fix his mind on the roads as they were then. Piles of horse dung. No motor-cars; no noise except a clip-clop and a jingle. What were the surfaces of the main roads like? He found he could not remember. But he could remember the sharp and delightful stink of horse, and the smell of leather.

For Dr. Holmes also the present pleasures were those of memory. Left alone by his rare gossips he would sit in the tea-shop or his untidy rooms, his pale eyes glazed over, looking back at his life.

Son of a Victorian clergyman with the expected full quiver, he had gone to Magdalen on scholarships, taken a brilliant first in Greats, and then a Fellowship at another college. His father to the end of his life believed Percival to be the success of the family. But Dr. Holmes knew better. He loved Greek, and was, he believed, next to Wilamowitz Möllendorf, the best living textual critic. He had kept his hands free from any of the vulgar popularizations such as those of the Regius Professor, Gilbert Murray. Indeed he had scored some severe hits on *that* school. He remembered with glee the time when he had told the professor that his last edition of Euripides deserved a place in the *Catena Classicorum*. Ha! That had been a bitter one. But deserved. If the *Classical Review* had dared to print his review, one reputation would have been finally ended. But what was the good of defending old style scholarship when Greek was nearly a forgotten language? He was like an alchemist or an astrologer, vainly offering instruction in sciences in which no one believed. He was lucky to receive only oblivion and not direct insult. *Nox est perpetua una dormienda*, but it was a little hard to be relegated to sleeping your perpetual night even before your death.

Worse still, his memory seemed to be failing. Adrian, Frederick, Lionel, Alistair… where were they, and which was which? There had never been any scandal, for nothing scandalous had ever occurred. They were all golden or dark boys, whom he had loved passionately, and who had elegantly supported his uncouth and obvious affection. For three years; and then, always, they had gone. Now their figures seemed to run into each other. He remembered walking tours, reading parties, holidays in Switzerland undertaken with his pupils; he saw himself clumsily clambering around rocks and suffering from sore feet, hating exercise but willing to suffer far worse than that to be allowed to go about with his favourite. He had controlled himself strictly, for he knew that he was far from attractive, and the university was old and well-informed. A little speculation about the Sacred Band of Thebes sometimes; sometimes to touch and at a great risk to kiss a hand; once or twice to say: "Do you know you're very handsome?" And by then it was generally too clear that he could go no further; and at the end of their third year they went away and forgot him.

Where were they now? Adrian, Maurice, Alistair, Lionel… some of them were dead. Handsome and young and dead…

eumorphoi... the enemy land has hidden its conquerors. The thought of
the war turned him suddenly away from Aeschylus to a memory
which had not dimmed. There had been, after all, one who had
not been indifferent to his shambling tutor. He had been allowed
to call him Dion. *Tears were fated for Hecuba and the Trojan women
as soon as they were born, but for you, Dion, when you had crowned
your success the gods poured out the finest hopes upon the ground; and
you have an honoured grave on the wide plains of your country. o Dion
who sent my heart mad with love.* "O emon ecmēnas thumon erōti,
Dion:" he whispered the line to himself again—the slightly too-
long dark curly hair and the bright brown eyes were before him
again, and the strong hand ruffled his own lanky strands. His
Dion had enlisted in 1914 in the R.F.C. and had come back within
a week broken. He lived three days in hospital, unconscious: he
was buried in the cemetery of the Wiltshire village where he was
born. *On the wide plains of his country.*

The only thing worth remembering in his life and that was
twenty-five years ago.

Dr. Holmes stood up dignifiedly in court despite his absurd
shape. The clerk had vexed him slightly by calling out the wrong
name but he repeated the oath in a loud firm voice: "I swear by
Almighty God that I will well and truly try, and true deliverance
make between our Sovereign Lord the King and the prisoner
at the bar whom I shall have in charge, and a true verdict give
according to the evidence."

Mr. Stannard, who had leapt up when his name had been called
and sat down again scarlet with shame, repeated the oath next,
stammering slightly and far from clearly.

4

The Clerk of Assize, his mind now firmly fixed on his duties, handed the Bible to the next juror and said: "Edward Bryan, repeat after me..."

HERE IS A PORTRAIT OF EDWARD BRYAN, FOURTH JUROR. At fifty-five he was a tall and melancholy-looking man, clean-shaven, with a narrow face, dark eyes and hair. He had a slight but perpetual twitch in the left eye which did not worry him because he was not aware of it. He was unmarried and occupied the post of cashier in an important branch of a large multiple grocery firm. He had occupied that post seventeen years and expected to continue to occupy it until he died or retired. Before he had been cashier he had been assistant cashier, before that he had served behind the counter, and before that he had been an errand boy, all for the same branch of the same firm. He had gone there immediately after leaving Board school and he had never attempted to go elsewhere. His mother had said to him: "Be respectful and hardworking, Edward; do your duty by Messrs. Allen and you'll never regret it." So he had done; not because of what his mother had said, for he had broken with her long before her death, but because it was in his nature. He was not unusually efficient, but he was industrious and silent: he had arrived at his present post chiefly by virtue of seniority.

He was neither liked nor disliked at his work; he was accepted almost as part of the furniture, he had been there so long. One of the girls in Cheese and Butter said that once when he was working late in his usual dark-grey suit a charwoman had dusted him without either of them noticing it. He never spoke to any of his fellow-workers, except in the way of business, when he addressed them with formal civility. He had no interest in sport, in women, in politics, in the condition of trade, or even in the conditions of work in the South-eastern Head Branch of Messrs. Allens. If attempts were made to open a conversation with him on any of these subjects, he repelled them by the use of a reply which had three forms, varying with the grade of the speaker:

(1) "I take no interest in such things. I would advise you to get on with your work."

(2) "I'm sorry, but the subject doesn't interest me."

(3) "I'm sorry, sir, but I know nothing about the subject. My interests have never lain in that direction."

So far as his colleagues knew, he had always "been that way". They left him alone after a while; he did no one any harm. Nor did they ever find out in which direction his interests did lie.

He had been that way for twenty-seven years: it was when he was twenty-eight that he settled into the way of life and thought which he never afterwards changed. Up till then he had been only a silent and rather clumsy young man, oppressed by the number of his family (he was one of nine children) and his obligation to help in supporting them.

He knew he was deficient in ambition and second-rate in intelligence. It cost him great efforts to perform his work adequately, and he was continually tired. He saw no hope of ever contributing much to help his family, and he did not very much like his family.

He was not so much miserable as discouraged; at so early an age he saw no meaning in life and felt as though he was weighted with burdens that were too heavy for him to carry and in which he had no interest. He did not like drinking and he did not like smoking; there was no relief for him there. Other relaxations he did not try. Indeed, the only signs of energy that he ever showed were sudden fits of rage in which he drew his lips back from his teeth and grinned like a dog. His family were frightened of him, not that he ever struck them but because his appearance was so ferocious. Moreover, he would break things—cups, a plate, or even the leg of a chair. Nor did he apologize after his fits; he merely ceased to rage.

These fits had also stopped at the age of twenty-eight, though that was of little help to his family, for he broke off all relations with them at the same time. After a certain day, when he left home, he never spoke to any of them again. When he received letters from them he read them carefully through, as though looking for something, tore them up and did not answer then. By now they had given up writing to him and he did not remember them very well; indeed, all his life before he had been twenty-eight was now half forgotten by him.

The change had come in him very suddenly, on a Sunday evening in March. He had on his bedroom wall one text which he had chosen because it seemed to him to promise relief from the burden which life was to him. It was from St. Matthew: chapter II, verse 28:

> *"Come unto me, all ye that labour and are heavy laden and I will give you rest."*

It seemed to him certain that if only he could interpret this aright he would find freedom from his load. But he had never been able to make it mean anything exact and certain; and the clergymen to whom he had listened had been useless. They had "offered only words", as he phrased it, for he thought in clichés. They had told him to be unselfish, to help others, and to be meek—in other words to go on in the same wretched dreary way that he was travelling. These were only words indeed, and words which were as obviously empty as that text was full of meaning, if he could only understand it.

Now, on that evening he was reading the First Epistle of St. Peter, and ever afterwards had a special affection for that small document, as one might have for an unimportant man who had put one in the way of an immensely profitable bit of business. The phrase which caught his attention and suddenly seemed to glow with meaning was not even a full sentence. It was from the tenth verse of the second chapter and ran:

"—which in time past were no people, but now are the people of God."

Who were these people? he asked himself. Then suddenly, almost with a click, he understood everything. His breath stopped, and then he gasped heavily, while his Bible slipped to the floor. He thought of falling on his knees, but could not wait to do so. This must be confirmed—confirmed at once, and he picked up the Bible and began to turn its pages again with frantic haste.

It was like finding the key word to a cross-word puzzle, the one which makes every other word suddenly plain. But Edward

Bryan never saw his revelation as anything so mundane as a cross-word puzzle. To him it invariably appeared as a narrow doorway streaming with light. All around him was darkness, in which there moved vaguely and uselessly, lumpish and unimportant, the things of this world. He could not see them clearly, nor did he wish to. Some ten feet away from him was a high and narrow slit, as from a door very slightly open, and through it was pouring a light so brilliant that nothing could be seen of what was beyond it. It was light and nothing else: it shone towards him not with a still radiance but with a sort of wavelike motion as if it were alive, and its goodness and warmth were ceaselessly being offered to him while he stood looking towards it. Some day, at an appointed time whose exact date did not matter to him, he would pass through that door; meantime when he lay awake in his bed he often would shut his eyes and peacefully watch that shining opening and let the beams beat restfully upon him.

It would have been surprising that others had not seen that light, if it had not been, as Scripture said, that they were literally blind. The truth was written out so patiently, so clearly, so much in words of one syllable that only blindness could explain their failure to see it. (And of course for blindness there was no cure: Edward Bryan was free of any need to proselytize.) The first text that he came to in his hurried search had been from St. Luke's parable of Dives and Lazarus:

> *"And beside all this, between us and you there is a great gulf fixed, that they that would pass from hence to you may not be able, and that none may cross from over thence to us."*

(He used, in every case, the Revised Version for greater safety.)

Parsons until then had repeated to him variegated versions of his mother's order to be good, and had said that this was Christianity. They had explained God as a force striving for betterness and helping us in self-improvement. Some had even talked politics and others had doubted about hell. All had concealed, or not known, the truth. But it was nevertheless written out repeatedly. He found another plain sentence:

> "He that believeth on the Son hath eternal life; but he that obeyeth not the Son shall not see life, but the wrath of God abideth on him." (St. John, iii, 36.)

There were (he saw) two wholly different kinds of person—the elect, who were very few, and of whom he was now one, and the wholly damned, who were innumerable. Judgment would come, and its character was quite explicitly indicated. His eye had fallen upon another passage in St. Matthew, which he copied out (ch. xxv.):

> "But when the Son of man shall come in his glory and all the angels with him, then shall he sit on the throne of his glory... Then shall he say also unto them on the left hand, Depart from me, ye cursed, into the eternal fire which is prepared for the devil and his angels."

There was very little doubt about the meaning of *that*: and yet there were priests and pastors who delivered sermons week after week completely unaware of this terrifying news. As if a man should announce earnestly and in exact terms that invasion and universal slaughter were imminent and then turn the conversation to the weather.

Even the numbers of the saved were known, and were recorded in the Book of Revelation, which became more and more Bryan's favourite reading.

> *"And I saw, and behold, the Lamb standing on the mount Zion, and with him a hundred and forty and four thousand having his name and the name of his Father written on their foreheads."*

A hundred and forty four thousand. 144,000. A thousand gross, as though it had been one of the entries that he continually checked for his employers. A celestial cashier, if the parallel was not too arrogant, was keeping the Divine books, and among the millions of this world a thousand gross were very few. It was hardly likely that he would find others of the elect.

Sometimes he attended a Four Square Gospel Chapel, or an extreme Evangelical sect; but he did not do so frequently. He doubted if the congregation were really the elect. He suspected their visible and violent excitement; consciousness of being elect should give calm. Anyway, he needed no confirmation from others; he relied confidently on his own interpretation of scripture.

Every night, as he closed his desk and took down his hat, he felt a silent relief, as if he was passing out of a grey and wet country into a sunny land. Before long he would be able once again to open his Bible, to see and feel the light; he said within himself, "I come, I come!" as if he had been crying to an impatient lover.

The flame was not always blazing. Undue attention to worldly things might dim it: some evenings he failed to see it at all when he had allowed himself to be too concentrated on his work or to be vexed by some external trouble or person. His friend, First Peter, explained to him why, in the verse that followed the one which had first enlightened him:

> *"Beloved, I beseech you as sojourners and pilgrims, to abstain from fleshly lusts which war against the soul."*

His soul was for him a machine to receive and record the heavenly light. It must be kept highly tuned and fit for duty. To abstain from fleshly lusts was not difficult for him. Drinking and smoking he had already effectively abandoned: now he made his rule rigid. He ate sparingly and drank water or cold milk instead of tea or coffee. He had no need to guard against love of fine raiments or the fascination of loose women. His new regime did not in the end differ greatly from the method of life he had already assumed, but as it was sparer it may be that he became definitely undernourished. It is certain that his spiritual life became more rather than less intense and his indifference to material conditions more marked.

The summons to serve upon a jury was something for which he was quite unprepared, and when he first received it he was displeased and unwilling. Fortunately, however, his perennial refuge did not fail him. First Peter, consulted, provided instructions exactly fitted to his need:

> *"Be subject,"* he read, *"to every ordinance of man for the Lord's sake: whether it be to the king, as supreme; or unto governors,*

as sent by him for vengeance on evildoers and for praise to them
that do well."

Momentarily, he flinched at the words in the oath: "Our Sovereign Lord the King." They seemed near to blasphemy, but the phrase of St. Peter, "the king, as supreme", remained in his mind and excused them, and he repeated the words with but a momentary hesitation.

5

While Mr. Bryan had been taking the oath, the Clerk had been covertly looking at the next juror. Courts were drab things, and a pretty woman was uncommon enough. Was this Mrs. Morris really pretty? Well, he wouldn't like to swear. Certainly she stood out like a single yellow flower in a green field among this dingy collection of mostly middle-aged men, with their grey or red faces. She had used scent fairly freely, and that was a better smell than the heavy dusty smell, as of old books, that filled the court. No doubt she was smart, though the Clerk would have been hard put to it to say what she wore. A blue coat and skirt and rather high heels would have been all that he could have sworn to, however great the need. But he was perfectly well aware of the general effect, and he almost had a paternal smile as he said: "Alice Rachel Morris: repeat after me…"

A LICE RACHEL WERE HER NAMES; ALICE BECAUSE SHE WAS modern and had given up all her racial beliefs and practices, Rachel because after all she was a Jewess from her too-high-heeled shoes to her bright and gleaming-eyed little face, so well made-up and so anxiously deprived of all individuality. And her happiest day, the day in one sense when life began for her, was when she stood before a registrar—refusing Jewish marriage—and said after him, "I, Alice Rachel Greenberg do take thee, Leslie Morris, for my lawful wedded husband." For all the devotion to family and sense of property that she could not or would not use as her fore-mothers had done, she concentrated on Les.

Her life, begun then, lasted two years: she was married at twenty-two and before she was twenty-five it was over. Half-Jews are unhappier than whole Jews: part of a nation, or a race, or whatever you choose to call it, was slowly assimilating itself to its neighbours until 1933, when it was ordered by Hitler to go back from where it came. Those who had never started on the journey were least injured; those who could no longer be Jews and might not now be Gentiles were the unhappiest. They were like chickens half out of the shell who were ordered back into the egg.

It was not by any means only in Germany and Italy that the order was given. Anti-Semitism is a contagion; indeed it is worse, it is an infection. Before Hitler came to power anti-Semitism had been an endemic disease only in certain limited areas where Jewish commercial competition was serious. Certain American towns, the environs of Stoke Newington and Whitechapel in London, for example. But in general in England and France, and in much of America and the British and French Empires, anti-Semitism did not exist in any serious form because its foundation did not exist. Men were not in the habit of asking themselves if their neighbours were Jews, not at least until they had asked many other questions first.

But once the Nazis had passed their laws and begun their pogroms even their enemies became Jew-conscious. The Scandinavian, the Frenchman, or the Englishman who had scarcely troubled himself about the matter began to examine his Jewish neighbours. The strongest anti-anti-Semite became, against his will, a Jew-smeller. Were Jews ill-mannered, rapacious, lustful, and dishonest? Did they congregate in loud-voiced, ostentatious groups? He must notice them more carefully, in order to refute these silly slanders. He defended Jews and so was only one degree less a pogromist than a Fascist; for he had ceased to look on them as normal human beings.

There is not, anthropologists tell us, any scientific basis whatever for Jew-smelling. Jews are not even a race: they are two, if not three different races, ethnologically indistinguishable from the communities from which they come. But this, though true, does not matter. Once any group, no matter what, is separated by a general suspicion or merely a general belief from the rest of society, it is by that mere fact made different, and develops at once marked characteristics of its own. These may not be the characteristics that its enemies believe—Herr Streicher's Jew is almost non-existent—but they are very real. So, since 1933, the Jews of England have become in fact more sharply differentiated from the Gentiles. They have developed more of both fearfulness and of compensating self-assertiveness. The anti-Semite lie has by its mere propagation brought into existence the differences on which it pretended to base itself.

Before Hitler, then, Les Morris would have passed unnoticed and unobjected-to among his fellows. No one would have considered that his shoes were too brightly polished, his ties too loud, his green shirts too fanciful, and the checks on his black and white suit too large. Or, if they did, they would merely have considered these clothes were the common sign of an East End upbringing, for the drabness of those acres of dreary streets must be compensated somehow, and what are easier than gaudy garments? They certainly could not have said that he looked like a typical Jew; for except to Rachel's eyes it is undeniable that he looked only like a fish, and very strikingly so. His complexion was of the pure and unvarying colour which distinguishes the underside of a plaice.

His mouth was perpetually half open, with that expression of astonished but respectful attention which is worn by a goldfish. His eyes were very pale and gave an erroneous impression of being unwinking. Nevertheless, after Hitler, people who had never seen him before could and did recognize him at sight as a Jew.

As against that, it must be put that almost every day his wife, as she watched him leave the home for the office, said under her breath: "But he is so handsome."

Early married life is the time for poetry; can there be any poetry more suited to Jews who are not Jews but consciously English than the verse of a Roman Catholic patriot? The Morrises' favourite was G. K. Chesterton. When they read,

> *The happy, jewelled alien men*
> *Worked then but as a little leaven;*
> *From some more modest palace then*
> *The Soul of Dives stank to Heaven.*

they knew that these words could not refer to them and their friends. They had no idea (no more than the writer) with what barbarisms words like these might turn out to be linked. But as they were too young to remember the disenchantment that followed 1914, it was war poetry which they liked most, and above all "The Wife of Flanders":

> *What is the price of that red spark that caught me*
> *From a kind farm that never had a name?*
> *What is the price of that dead man they brought me?*
> *For other dead men do not look the same.*

How should I pay for one poor graven steeple
 Whereon you shattered what you shall not know?
How should I pay you, miserable people?
 How should I pay you everything you owe?

The end to this came very suddenly, and for no reason and following no pattern, as evil things generally do. Or at least for very little reason and if there was any pattern it was one too great for the Morrises' life to fit into it. Les had a third share in a timber firm; it was doing very well and there were no warnings of trouble. Indeed that very morning, a Sunday, they had gone up to Golder's Green to look at houses, for the time seemed to be coming when they could move out to a really nice district. In the afternoon they walked out to see an aunt in Whitechapel: she lived in one of the streets off the north of the High Street. It was a hot, dry, fine afternoon, and the side streets were as empty as the main street was full. Hardly any one about except a few yobos who had got nothing to do, and hung around in irritated idleness, spitting manfully in the gutter and telling dirty stories which they all had heard before.

Danny Leary was seventeen and had had no regular employment since he left school. Neither had most of his gang—if gang be not too dignified a word. They were more a casual group whose only common bond was a habit of destructive mischief. They did not carry knives and when they fought, which was frequently, they used feet and hands. Most were pretty much the same age and strength; Sammy Redfern was the youngest and smallest, tolerated for a peculiar ability of reproducing without moving his lips all the less polite noises of the human body. This greatly brightened conversation, especially with his elders. There were times when quite important persons had been discomposed by a prolonged and resonant rumble appearing to come from their own interior.

Five of the boys had hung round the corner of Burdett Road, "accidentally" pushing the passers-by and calling out meaningless cries until it seemed that the police had noticed them. Then they drifted slowly westwards along Mile End road. Near the People's Palace they caught sight of two girls they knew, walking along equally aimlessly, in the uncertain hope of some unspecified "bit of fun". Danny and Frank, a young man of about his age, crossed the road and raised their hats with an exaggerated gesture.

"Going anywhere, Rosie dear?" said Danny.

"Walky talky with me?" was Frank's effort.

Such wit deserved and received a high giggle. "Well, I reelly don't know," said Rosie.

"What about Victoria Park?"

"What about the pictures?"

"Oh, come on, you c'n have more fun in the park."

"Marlene Dietrich's on at the Rivoli."

There was a deadlock and then Rosie made her decision. "Come *on*, Lil. They haven't got the price of a seat between them, I dessay. Wouldn't spend it if they had. The Something-for-Nothing brigade as usual."

"Wouldn't spend it on you anyway," was all Frank could manage as they passed on.

Sammy produced a monster eructation, and was kicked on the ankle for his pains. "Play the fool when you're asked to," said Danny.

They had spent another hour completely aimlessly when they turned into a street north of Whitechapel High Street. It happened to be the street in which the Morrises were walking. A flicker of life came into them.

"Let's have a bit of fun with the shonks," said Frank.

They made a procession in the gutter near the Morrises, one gibbering, flapping his hands and dragging his feet like a stage Hebrew, Sammy making the obscenest noises he could near to Alice, Danny and Frank speculating loudly about Les's performance as a husband, the rest singing a song whose words were clear.

The Morrises, though their colour heightened, took no notice. Danny got angry; this was no fun. "'Ere," he said to his crowd. "This way."

They bolted down a side street, led by Danny, turned right, ran round the block and came to the end of the street down which the Morrises were walking. They linked arms and walked towards the Morrises, all now singing the song.

The Morrises crossed to the other side of the road. They crossed, too.

The two lines came together—five youths, facing a man and his wife. Alice was trembling and Les was uneasy. But after all this was London, not Berlin, and he was an Englishman.

"Please let us pass," he said in a firm voice.

"Oo-hoo! You kikes *going* anywhere?" said Danny with falsetto surprise.

"Will you let us pass?"

"Naughty! Naughty! Temper!" Frank's wit was reviving. He slipped his hand loose, tweaked Les's tie out of his waistcoat and flipped it into his face. "Muck you shonks wear," he added.

Les, white and breathing fast, pushed the tie back. There was no use, anyway, in running away, even if that had been the thing to do with hooligans. "Let me pass," he said and thrust forward. Danny gave him a huge push back, and Frank slapped his wrist.

"You ——s need a lesson," said Danny in a suddenly thick voice, and hit him on the shoulder.

Les was no coward and he was wiry. He hit straight out and caught Danny on the end of his nose, a very painful kind of blow. Now both Frank and Danny rushed at him, using feet as well as hands. Les's fists whirled round like flails, till Sammy kicked him neatly and viciously in the muscle behind the knee. He went down with a thump, and Frank knelt on his face. Alice clawed at the louts' backs, and kicked at them with her small pointed shoes, squealing shrilly. In a few seconds they had finished: Les's clothes were torn, his face running with blood, someone had stamped on his hand. As he rose, Danny deliberately aimed at him a savage kick in the side of the belly.

"Get art, you," he said.

He watched them stagger away silently, Les almost unable to stand and leaning on Rachel. His lower jaw dropped and his tongue hung out slightly; he seemed to be thinking. "Cheese it now," he said after a minute to the gang. "They'll fetch the cops."

They ran down the side street and scattered. Danny found himself with Sammy. "Cor," shrilled the smaller boy, almost dancing along. "That *was* fine. That shonk didn't half cop it. See his face?"

"Shut up!" said Danny and hit him an angry blow on the side of his neck. Sammy took a single look at his expression and became dead silent.

★

Les felt very ill and they decided not to go to his aunt's but straight back home to lie down. Alice washed his wounds and he said he would soon be better. But that evening he began to vomit blood. The doctor was called. He said it was a ruptured spleen—definitely a dangerous case—night and day nurse—no possibility of moving him. Les fell into a coma and died three days later without speaking.

For other dead men do not look the same.

Alice Morris could not even have revenge. The police searched with anxious zeal, for they feared this modern Mohockery as much as any one, and knew more than any one how common it was becoming. But Alice could tell them so pitifully little. She could not even be sure of recognizing the gang, and she had not heard the names of a single one. She was shown several "possibles": not one was right.

In the end the police gave it up. She still lived on Les's money and in Les's house, for the business went on. But she hardly cared whether she lived or not, and when the jury notice came, paid it very little attention. A bit sardonic, she thought, when she was finally chosen. The law did nothing to protect *me,* and now expects me to protect and punish others. It wants my time, it claims it as a debt, and it wouldn't do anything to save Les. How shall I pay it everything it owes? But what does it matter? Do what it wants. Say the words that it wants.

So in her turn she stood up in court, kissed the book, and said in a flat, clipped monotone:

"I swear by Almighty God…"

6

Experienced Clerks of Assize have the equivalent of a pineal eye. They know if behind them a judge or high officer of the court moves or changes his expression. This Clerk suddenly becomes aware that Sir Isambard Burns, leading for the defence, had lifted his eyebrows. A cold fear that he might be "spoken to" overcame him. Till now he had indulged himself by administering the oath slowly and inspecting the juror. He had better brisk himself up. Supposing he was publicly told to hurry up! He gabbled the oath and pushed the remaining jurors through at twice the speed.

"Edward Oliver George, repeat after me…"

"Francis Arthur Horder Allen, repeat after me…"

"David Elliston Smith, repeat after me…"

"Ivor William Drake, repeat after me…"

"Gilbert Parham Groves, repeat after me…"

"Henry Wilson, repeat after me…"

THE SIX MEN SO UNCEREMONIOUSLY HUSTLED THROUGH were for the most part of medium height and undistinguished appearance. "First Citizen, second Citizen, third Citizen…" At first sight an observer might have taken them for genuine Mr. Zeroes, typical specimens of suburban inhabitants, supplied to order by a celestial department store. Only a closer inspection showed a marked difference in age, and a closer knowledge would have shown an even greater difference in disposition.

Edward Oliver George was the oldest. His face was tired; he looked and was over fifty. Inconspicuously dressed in a dark suit, he managed to wear his Sunday best as if it was his habit to go about in good clothes. His thoughts were far away from the Court, away even from the small house which contained his wife and three children, a credit to him (as he considered) on six pounds a week. His thoughts stayed wholly in his office. He had only been General Secretary of the National Union of Plasterers' Labourers for two years, and even now was not sure that the heartbreaking disorder created by his predecessor had been wholly cleared up. When he came in there had been an overdraft at the bank and the records were in depressing confusion. Men were drawing benefit who were not entitled to it: more, one branch secretary had even drawn strike pay for seven dead members. The first thing to be done had been to get the Executive to enforce the rule book strictly. That had been no easy job, and he had made many enemies. At one branch meeting two of his critics had set on him and he had thought for a minute that his time was up. Plasterers' labourers can be very tough. But the branch had rallied to him: he was an elderly man and till a year or so ago had worked on a job like all the rest of them, and they would not see him knocked about. The meeting ended in an overwhelming vote of confidence in his policy, and an abrased nose for one of his critics.

Next it had been his task to persuade the Society to abandon its vendetta against other building trade workers and join up with the National Federation of Building Trade Operatives. This had been an easier task in reality, though it had seemed a greater. The enforcing of the rule book had already taken out of the hands of the members their power to start V.T. continual small strikes over "demarcation disputes." With the disappearance of these the chief occasion of quarrels with other unions vanished. The motion to affiliate to the Federation had been carried on a poll by 16,401 to 5,003 votes, and the newly elected Executive had duly made application. And now, just at this moment, with an untried executive and an important job like this on hand, there must needs come this stupid piece of paper calling him away from his work! That very morning he had had a note on his desk from the collecting steward on Trollope & Colls's new job saying there'd be trouble any minute. No one in the office except the girl and the new chairman of the executive, who could hardly write his own name. Mr. George received the instruction to repeat the oath with an undisguised scowl. To have to sit all day listening to stuff that didn't concern him; and Heaven knows what would be done behind his back. He'd told the girl to hold back all letters: he'd have to work half the night because of this imposition. "... give according to the evidence." He very nearly slammed the Bible down as he finished.

"Francis Arthus Horder Allen."

The man who succeeded him was obviously much younger, though he looked more than his twenty-six years. Something in his dress and way of standing showed that he was but recently down from Oxford or Cambridge. Dr. Holmes turned and looked at him: a don is not deceived. If he had known anything of his precursor's occupation and interests, Allen would have claimed that they two were the only representatives of the workers on the jury. Yet there can have been no other two men on the jury who would have understood each other less.

Black hair, dark eyes, a thin and incessantly excited face, Francis Allen was the most restless and probably the happiest man on the jury, except perhaps Edward Bryan. Can there be any greater happiness than to be young, unworried by money troubles, filled with desire to reform the world, knowing that you know the way, and married recently to a young woman with whom you are in love? This is a portmanteau picture of Francis Allen, as he was when he stood up and took the oath. He had changed very quickly—he was only three years from the young examinee on the Classical Tripos who told his friends that the sole object of all education was to be able to read and understand Spinoza. He thought that young man a prig and a fool: he was certain that that phase was over and that his present metamorphosis was his last. He did not hold a Communist Party ticket: he was not quite sure why he had held back. But after Spinoza he had read Marx—a great deal of Marx, after Marx some of Lenin, and after Lenin a very little Stalin, for by then his appetite for this literature was sated. For his Socialism or Communism (he varied the word according to his company) was not economic in origin, but emotional: his real teachers were Auden, Isherwood, Lewis and Spender, and if he had not been afraid of being unfashionable they would have been Shelley and Swinburne, too. He had written poetry himself, but he had the good sense to see the verses were imitations of Auden and they remained unpublished, except for two poems which had appeared in the *Left Review.*

He had been married six months; he called her Jenny, because they both agreed that Caroline Dorothy was intolerable. And for this year and many years to come his two loves were one love: her thoughts and hopes were his: as he lived and fought and sacrificed for the Cause, so he loved and fought and sacrificed for her. Speaking at meetings, patrolling the streets, chalking the pavements, picking quarrels with the Fascists, defying police tyranny (but never yet had he had a real fight), he always felt that she was with him, approving and supporting, as often she was in the flesh. Loving her, feeling her head on his shoulder, listening to her tired, contented breathing, he was not a warrior deserting the field, but a comrade seeking and giving strength, uniting himself more closely with his fellow warrior and doubling both their power.

> *Vivamus, mea Lesbia, atque amemus*
> *Rumoresque senum severiorum*
> *Omnes unius aestimemus assis.*

"Let's live and love, my Lesbia, and reckon at a penny all the mutterings of conservative old men." He had taught her just enough Latin to follow Catallus's love songs.

> *Da mi basia mille, deinde centum*
> *Dein mille altera, dein secunda centum.*

"Give me a thousand kisses, then a hundred, then another thousand, then a second hundred." He would go through the whole poem, aloud or under his breath: he knew no English words that would carry his meaning.

This very morning he had been woken early by the sun coming in through uncurtained windows. The curtains were never drawn since he had read a sentence from John Wilkes's story of his tour through Italy with Gertrude Corradini: "There were no curtains," wrote the eighteenth century gallant, "a circumstance in so temperate a climate most agreeable to Mr. Wilkes, because every sense was feasted in the most exquisite degree, and the visual ray held sometimes in contemplation the two noblest objects of creation, the glory of the rising sun and the perfect form of naked beauty." His visual ray had to be cheated, for Jenny complained at the bedclothes being pulled off. "Must you love me so coldly?" The gradual lightening of the room gave him a slower and more sure pleasure. At first all was grey and uncertain: gradually outlines became clear, and then colours followed them. Over across the room were his books. A big orange patch, part standing and part fallen, were Left Book selections—the later ones, unfortunately, unread. Then a white patch—pamphlets. A red group: that was *Capital,* whose title would soon be legible. A long shelf below, irregular and of all colours; that was full of his Latin and Greek books. Not until all these were brilliantly clear would he allow himself to look at the dark head beside his on the pillow. And only after he had watched that still head until his breath was faster and the muscles of his face had tightened, as a baby's do when it is going to cry, would he allow his hand to touch the smooth skin next to him. And then, he knew, the figure would turn itself round, swing a white arm out from the bedclothes across his body, and, eyes still closed in sleep, put up a half-pouting mouth to be kissed.

So this day he attended in court, strong not weak after love, with such memories in the background of his mind. In the foreground was an intense curiosity: shortly, he thought, there was to be played before him a drama to which he alone held the key. Capitalist society had manufactured a highly complex machine to protect itself, and he was to see its workings from the inside. He knew too little of the legal system; it would be good to know how it really worked. He might be going to see corruption and oppression, the crushing of an individual. Or he might merely be going to be shown a picture of the decay of bourgeois life, a miniature of the death of a once powerful society. He took the oath negligently, not paying any attention to the words, and settled down to watch.

"David Elliston Smith."

Mr. Elliston Smith was as ordinary as a man can be without being a caricature. He could have been Mr. Strube's Little Man if he had only been undersized instead of normal height. He wore a bowler and a small moustache; he did not carry an umbrella only because the weather was fine and likely to stay so. He considered that he had been called up for jury service in error, but there was nothing that he could do about it. He was only technically a householder; but he *was* technically, and that settled the matter. He was one of four young men who had clubbed together, for economy's sake, to take one of the new houses on a building estate. It had three bedrooms and two sitting-rooms. The front room was turned into a bedroom and the back room—opening on the garden and with French windows—kept as a common room. So everybody had a room of his own. A woman came in to do for them and get an evening meal; the resultant expense was less than each one taking digs, and they had a house of their own and no one to interfere with them. No spying landladies. Elliston Smith had originally had misty thoughts of wild freedom, of "orgies" with complaisant young women, and drunken revellers lying in heaps on the cushions. Nothing like that had occurred yet, though he had not abandoned hope. Their combined resources did not run to more than bottled beer, and the few girls he knew were impregnably respectable and not in the least mysterious and seductive.

The building society had declined to accept four young men as mortgagees. Some one person had to be entered as owner, and Elliston Smith was chosen. He was assistant in a well-established hairdressers', and his employers were prepared to give him a cautious reference. He was twenty-four years old, unmarried and unattached, not a teetotaller but abstemious, friendly towards his parents, who lived in Dalston, but independent of them, a Conservative but a member of the League of Nations Union (in arrears), a supporter of Mr. Winston Churchill and of the Arsenal, a cinema-goer and a disliker of Jews without being in any way vehement. He took the oath with considerable pleasure, being a reader of detective stories and expecting scenes of thrilling excitement. It did not occur to him that he might be going to be abominably bored.

"Ivor William Drake."

Mr. Drake held the book gracefully, he was conscious that he was well posed, he rebuked himself for being conscious, and then rebuked himself for rebuking himself. After all, if a man was an actor he should *be* an actor. There was no sense in shuffling and clumping about the place when you could move with dignity, and with an awareness of the fact that a life might shortly depend upon your decision.

All the same that was, he reflected, likely to be the trouble right through the case. Every pose of counsel, every trick of movement or expression of the defendant, would be to him nothing but a pose or a trick. He would estimate it just as he would have done in a theatre—good acting, bad acting, or passable. Confound it, could he never be sincere, nor even recognize sincerity? A half-humorous grimace of irritation, as good as any of Noel Coward's, ran across his face.

Mr. Ivor Drake (he dropped the William) was twenty-seven years old, and he had decided to be an actor at the age of nine, when a tipsy uncle had taken his to see Owen Nares. He still could see the scene: Mr. Nares had been acting *à deux* with a well-known actress whose name had vanished. Hooey? Iris Hoey? His mind settled on that like a fly and then flitted away. Never mind: Owen Nares had shouted at her and looked so handsome. He remembered her smile as she turned to leave. "Bully me again, dear," she had said, and then the lights went suddenly out. Nowadays, he was inclined to believe that that music-hall turn had been a sort of prenatal influence, and a bad one. For now he looked back on it, he did not think Owen Nares had acted at all. He had stood about and been handsome; nothing more. And for years after he had decided to act Mr. Drake had underacted. He had stood about and been as handsome as he could manage.

At the Oxford University Dramatic Society he had imitated Gerald du Maurier till even the devotees protested. He could tap a cigarette and mumble exactly like their idol; he could sing a little light music rather huskily in a fair imitation of Mr. Coward; but he could do no more. When he came to London his father's allowance kept him from starving, and the fact that he was in the fashion found him a few small parts.

But he was earnest in his profession, and not a fool. Du Maurier was dead and his dazzling charm no longer spoiled a whole generation of young actors. Drake woke suddenly. Too suddenly, perhaps: he now overacted. He was always playing Elizabethan. He told his friends that acting was a science, not an art, though what he meant by that was not clear. He would spend an hour or more before a mirror studying his own face, posing in very odd postures, and watching his expression. He made notes with numbers attached, indicating the position of every movable feature—eyebrows, eyes, lips—on a geographical chart, with latitude and longitude marked as on a map. The line of his nose was 0° and his right ear W. and his left E. By this means he had acquired a large file of cards, on which were marked the best possible expressions for indicating every common emotion, in degrees of strength running from one to ten. They were his most treasured possessions: he had shown them to one or two friends but they had been ribald. Now he kept them locked in his desk, but he practised with them assiduously before every rehearsal.

"Gilbert Parham Groves."

There was a curious similarity between these two jurors: even the Clerk of Assize delayed his hurry sufficiently for a quick darting look. Their suits seemed identical—well cut, single breasted, dark grey. They looked, and were the same age; their height was identical, and both moved with the smooth, easy gait that every tailor associates with the well-dressed and well-bred young man. They both had ruddy faces, blue eyes, fairly clean-cut features, and no moustache.

But the resemblance was only superficial. Mr. Drake was what he acted, Mr. Groves only wished to be. Money and Oxford had given Mr. Drake his carriage: Mr. Groves had learnt it by watching models. For Mr. Groves was one of a very unfortunate caste:

he was a gentleman travelling salesman. He had escaped from vacuums, it is true, but all those rackets are much the same. You go from door to door, exaggerating grossly the merits of your goods, knowing that you are lying. You are fairly sure that your customers can't afford what you offer and don't need it. You must look prosperous and a gentleman, and yet be prepared to be insulted and have doors slammed in your face. Unless you are going to sink slowly and miserably down until you end in the Spike, you have got to cultivate the qualities which the noisy bounder who engages you shows most perfectly. You have to have a brass finish. You must have no shame, you must be insistent against every canon of good taste, you must bully at need, you must be literally untiring, and above all you must never stop talking once you have trapped a listener. You must in short have all the qualities of a dictator, except that you had better know nothing about politics.

Mr. Groves had most of these qualifications, and what he had not he was being forced to acquire. Like most of his fellow workers, he was a child of lower middle-class parents who had found that the industrial organization that had provided reasonably well for his father had no room for him and tens of thousands like him. His father and mother had sent him to a private school instead of a secondary school. State schools, they considered, were for the common people; at St. Desmond's College the *tone* was so nice. The headmaster was so agreeable, too, and one felt safer always with a clergyman, didn't one? The school cap, school tie, and school blazer—crimson and royal blue—might have been those of a real public school; Mr. and Mrs. Parham Groves never inquired into the qualifications of the staff that the Rev. Mr. Bowindow had assembled nor even into the equipment of such things as the science lab. The school seemed as good or better than those of their own youth, and much more gentlemanly. The unfortunate Gilbert left school, in consequence, hardly half as well educated as the "county schoolcads", and without either qualifications for or prospects of a job.

Mr. Parham Groves, senior, by using to the utmost his old connections with the City, got him the only steady employment of his life. It was as a clerk in a firm of outside brokers, doing a small business but a perfectly honest one. He was there for just over a year; the firm did not survive the 1931 slump. Since then he had lived as best he could, with frequent help from his parents. He could play tennis well; he never read a book; he typed and did office work fairly well; he was quarrelsome because he was unhappy; he was not intelligent, though he was unmalicious and willing to work if he could only have been directed. That he was slowly rotting was none of his fault.

Nowadays he was selling *Campbell's Universal Encyclopedia*, twelve volumes, on the instalment system. It was ten years out of date, though it was not a bad publication in itself. Moreover it had a good name: earlier, Victorian editions, written and edited mostly by Scotsmen who had been under the influence of Darwin and one or two actually taught by Huxley, had justly secured it a household reputation. The British public is faithful to the point of imbecility: it continued to buy *Campbell's* because Grandfather had admired it when he was young.

But the market had been saturated, and Mr. Parham Groves had been among the first sent out to try a new technique. The owners of *Campbell's* had brought out a new publication, *Campbell's*

Annual, which consisted of short articles of a popular kind, on the advance of science, literature and art during the year, completed by a Diary of Great events, and a large selection of news photographs. This they priced at 30s.: it was not doing well.

Mr. Parham Groves was given a list of addresses, with a note against each name of the victim's occupation and telephone number. Then he began the campaign according to instructions. His first prospect: was a Mr. Prittwell, whom he rang on the telephone:

"May I speak to Mr. Prittwell?"

*

"Mr. Prittwell?"

*

"You won't know my name; it's Groves. Parham Groves. But I'm the bearer of good news—at least, I think you'll think it is, ha, ha! The directors of *Campbell's Universal Encyclopedia* have decided to present you with a copy of our latest edition, specially bound."

*

"Oh, no, no,; nothing like that. It's a *presentation* copy, made to a few selected persons only. May I call round to-morrow and explain it?"

*

"Four o'clock to-morrow? Thank you."

Mr. Groves arrived exactly on time, with the air of a well-to-do person about to confer a favour. He found Mr. Prittwell a middle-aged worried man in charge of a typing agency.

"We've decided, Mr. Prittwell," he said with a brilliant smile, "on a wholly new kind of publicity. *Campbell's* is known to everybody, of course; but that is not enough. It can only have the sale it deserves if a few people in key positions who really need it, and can use it properly, are *seen* using it. If people, like yourself, who influence others, find it their standby. What is the good of it to us—to anybody—to the world-famous scholars who have given it of their very best, if it lies idly collecting dust upon the shelves? We have decided, therefore, to *give* a number of copies to persons in key positions. I admit to you frankly that it is a publicity device. It's fortunate for those persons who have been chosen as recipients, but of course we hope it will do us a bit of good, too. We make no conditions but that the book should be *used*."

Mr. Prittwell made an indeterminate answer. He was flattered, eager for a free copy, but still suspicious.

"I hope you won't mind me asking you—quite confidentially, of course," said Mr. Groves, man to man, "for a brief account of what you do, and the kind of people you meet. Just to satisfy my directors."

Mr. Prittwell now was sure that the offer was a serious one. He outlined his business, enlarged it, and exaggerated the contacts which it brought him. Mr. Parham Groves watched him admiringly, and said at the end:

"Well! I can see clearly why the directors picked upon you as one of the favoured few. Very natural, and very proper. I think we may call that settled.

"There's only one further point. As I said, we want to be sure the books are *used*. And kept up to date. I presume you know *Campbell's Annual*, our remarkable new enterprise?"

"Well—er—I'm afraid not," said Mr. Prittwell, apologizing.

"I haven't a copy here." (Curiously enough, Mr. Parham Groves never had a copy, either of that or of the big *Encyclopedia*). "But

I have binding specimens." He unfolded a curious sort of cardboard concertina, on which were stuck the backs of *Annuals* of various dates.

"We just want to make sure that you take this invaluable supplement regularly, to help the *Encyclopedia,* which is a free gift, up to date. You would give us an order for the next ten issues, which would be delivered to you in due course, post paid."

Mr. Prittwell had begun to hesitate.

"But I don't think," he said, "I want to commit myself to payments so far ahead. Ten years! Fancy paying all that time."

"Oh, naturally not," said Mr. Parham Groves. "You would pay us in advance."

"How much?" A slightly different tone had come into Mr. Prittwell's voice.

"Merely thirty shillings each issue. A magnificent book. Written by the same world-famous scholars, and by our unequalled staff..." Mr. Groves talked hard and quick; but Mr. Prittwell had begun to calculate.

"Ten thirty shillingses," he said. "That's fifteen pounds. And I can get a good clean copy of your *Encyclopedia* anywhere for ten."

He suddenly found wrath in his mouth. This popinjay—that was the word, popinjay—had slouched into his office, cross-examined him about his business, and fooled him into believing in a gift scheme. Him, a business man! He rose to his full inconsiderable height and interrupted Mr. Parham Groves.

"Get out!" he shouted.

Mr. Groves left the room, slowly, and with an expression of contempt.

His life was a steady repetition of such scenes. One time in seven he would plant a set. Then he would get his commission. He had a token salary of 15s. otherwise.

Now, when he had just got started, he was called up for a jury service. Damned nonsense. Still, it would be a rest, and it would be something to talk about at the tennis club. He took the oath mechanically.

"Henry Wilson."

Henry Wilson bounced forward, pleasant and cheerful, and as brisk as the clerk. The press was always on the spot, even an organ as small as the *Primrose Hill Argus*. Man and boy, he'd been on that paper thirty years, and it hadn't changed. It was a steadier and more permanent feature of the British press, to his mind, than plenty of papers that put on airs in Fleet Street. He had looked at some numbers of the 1890s—why, bar the advertisements, they might have been edited by him. The same solid grey slabs of text, about the council meetings, the performances of the Amateur Dramatic Societies, the police court cases, the street improvements, the editor's jottings, the correspondence. Of course, to-day, there were some changes. The theatre notices were replaced by cinema notes, provided by the local managers and scarcely changed. There was a woman's page, run by "Lass of Primrose Hill", and consisting mostly of regurgitated hints from old cookery and housekeeping books. The political meetings were rather different and he didn't report sermons any more.

He had two reporters and a sub-editor under him, with some extra help sometimes on Thursday, which was press day. A lot of copy came in free: schools were only too anxious to report their own prize-givings and dramatic societies their performances. Political meetings had to be covered: as much as possible he did this himself. He would give Labour just a little less prominence than Conservatives: Liberals were almost extinct. "Pressmen have no politics," he always told inquirers. "Like Caesar's wife, you know." In his editor's jottings he mildly favoured the Conservative councillors and gently criticized the Socialists, and always ended with a placatory phrase ascribing good will to every one.

He was forty-six, and unmarried, lived with his married sister and was devoted to her six children. They called him Uncle Harry and were boisterously fond of him: he was inclined to excite them too much and make them nuisances. He liked company; he belonged to the Buffaloes, the Druids, and the Oddfellows; on Friday nights he took rather too much beer. He was the last juror and quite unconsciously smacked his lips as he finished the oath.

7

FROM THE JURY-BOX, THEY ALL LOOKED FIRST AND MOST consistently at one spot. Even Mr. Popesgrove, the most meticulous about his behaviour, saw no reason why he should not gaze steadily at the figure in the dock. They saw a middle-aged woman, dressed in black, with a white collar. The women noticed that her nails were not coloured, but had nail polish on them. The hands were rather fattish and had not done housework for many years; they fidgeted continually. The dock prevented any clear view of her clothing: it seemed decent without being distinctive. The face was that of a middle-aged woman, not heavily powdered and with only a touch of lipstick. The hair was fair and long. Mrs. Morris looked at it and wondered idly if its colour was natural. Probably not, she considered. No one else troubled about it.

The face? Nose rather too beaky, heavy lines from it to a down-drawn mouth. Eyes red and tired; and she would not look at the jury. Her glance roamed to and fro about the court. Indeed, you could deduce nothing about her from her expression, except that she was frightened. Mr. Stannard had hoped that he might be able to judge the accused, whoever he or she might be, on his or her looks and manner. As he judged customers in his bar, and as he would once have judged a horse; and mind you, he could remember how to judge a horse. That would have helped him, for he very much doubted if he could follow evidence. But this woman's face and stance told him nothing.

Nor were the rest of the figures in court more informative to the eye as the jurors looked round. All men in wigs and gowns at first sight look like puppets. The room seemed full of marionettes. The judge looked like a shrivelled and malicious doll made from leather. Sir Isambard Burns, the chief counsel for the defence, had a thin long body and a crowlike face. Into one eye he continually fitted and removed an eyeglass: he looked like a Christmas toy performing a tedious trick. Counsel who was now rising for the Crown looked like a wax doll: his shiny pink face under his wig looked as unreal as if it had been painted.

Mr. Stannard had gobbled his breakfast and he was suffering badly from nerves. Before counsel could speak his fate overcame him, and he was publicly shamed, as he had been sure would occur somehow. A vast hiccup caught him unawares, and a sound like *twirp* thundered through the court. He turned scarlet, and devoted his attention to repressing his diaphragm.

Mr. Bertram Proudie, about to begin his speech for the prosecution, looked at this white-haired and red-faced juror with open disapproval. After a minute's hesitation he began a set oration. He conveyed to the jurors that they were about to try a case of the gravest possible nature. No other charge compared in seriousness with the one which was about to be set before them. For this was a charge of murder.

The court had already begun to settle back into an atmosphere of resigned tedium. One of Proudie's usual long-winded introductions was on the way. Only Mr. Stannard seemed ill at ease. His face grew purple and sweat-beads stood out on it; he was struggling with his diaphragm. But it would not do; if you have the hiccups, the hiccups will win, resist how you may.

Right in the middle of a forty-word sentence it came, louder than ever: *Twirp!*

Mr. Proudie flushed, but went on with his discourse, going from the general to the particular so far as to note that the accused was a married woman, a widow, by name Rosalie Van Beer, but apart from that still keeping to the consideration of general principles. Mr. Stannard, his nerve wholly shattered, bent his head down and appeared to be rustling papers between his legs, presumably overcome with shame.

He had, however, an unsuspected plan. As those who suffer from this nervous trouble know, there is but one ready method of stopping it, and that is to breathe in carbon dioxide, which paralyses the diaphragm. Carbon dioxide is not readily available but it is the main content of the breath which you breathe out. Mr. Stannard was about to take advantage of this information. He had just remembered that his lunch was in his attaché case, and that it was contained in a large brown paper bag. He was extracting this bag, and when he had done so straightened himself up relievedly. Then, with innocent gravity and good faith, as he would have done at home, and as he had always been taught to do, he concealed his face in the bag and breathed heavily in and out.

Mr. Proudie stopped dead. The court stared appalled. The judge, who probably feared that Mr. Stannard was demented and was about to blow out the bag and burst it with a loud pop, was the first to speak. "Will the fourth juror," he said sharply, "be kind enough to explain his conduct?" The fourth juror, highly discomposed, removed the bag and opened his mouth to obey; but once again was caught. *Twirp!* he said involuntarily; and then added, despairing of explaining, "Will your lordship excuse me a minute?"

"We will await your return," said the judge coldly.

Cold water, and the use of his chosen remedy in the corridor restored Mr. Stannard. When he returned to the jury box, shaken and humble, Mr. Proudie resumed. But the juror's eccentric behaviour had completely destroyed his exordium. The court benefited by Mr. Stannard's affliction, for Mr. Proudie now went straight to his story, and told it, as he could when he chose, lucidly and without rhetoric.

These were the events which he now began to summarize...

PART II

The Case

"**S**REDNI VASHTAR?" SAID MRS. ROSALIE VAN BEER, LOOKING suspiciously at her eleven-year-old nephew Philip. "Sredni Vashtar? What made you give the rabbit a name like that?"

The child looked back at her cunningly and not too pleasantly. "It oughtn't to be a rabbit," was all he would say.

Mrs. van Beer scowled at him. She thought of telling him again that what she hated above all in a child was secretiveness and evasion. Any boy who had nothing to conceal would always be *honest* and *direct*. Frank confession of a fault would generally bring forgiveness (she usually went on, never suspecting Philip's unspoken but unvarying comment that he had been caught once that way). But evasiveness was an impertinence and made things worse. However, this time she decided to say nothing. She wasn't sure of her ground; she merely resented the odd name as she resented anything that she did not understand. She hardly ever read a book; her reading was almost confined to the *Daily Minor,* the *Sunday Pictorial,* and one other Sunday paper.

She gave up the problem for the moment and stood in the French window looking at her nephew playing on the lawn with a brindled buck rabbit whom till now she had believed to be named King Zog. She had no love for it anyway; it had bitten her sharply the day before when she was teasing it ("playing with it," she said) in its hutch. She wondered whether it would not be best to forbid the keeping of pets altogether. She would consult Dr. Parkes on his next visit. Very many diseases could be carried by animals: parrots killed people by a special illness of their own and rats brought plague. Quite likely Philip's health demanded it. Mrs. van Beer began to feel more cheerful. A prohibition, for Philip's own good, generally had that effect on her, though she had never realized it and would have been immensely indignant if any one had said so.

She reflected, as she watched her nephew, that all her thought and unremitting kindness seemed to have had little effect. She did not expect gratitude. Oh, no, she never expected any *reward*. She knew too well what human nature was. (Her mind rattled along like an empty goods train: the phrases that she was using would be worked off upon the sympathetic Dr. Parkes.) But it was surprising that Philip should be such a poor specimen of a *boy*. So skinny and yellow, short-sighted, weak, and querulous. Always complaining, not eating his food, and with those stupid little fits of rage. Not a nice companion for children of his own age even.

Mrs. van Beer did not reflect that her own rules prevented his going out except on very rare occasions ("he gets so excited") and that the few times that he had had visitors she had stayed with the children and regulated the games herself.

"Don't let that rabbit escape," she said to him, and turned from the garden into the house. She found Mrs. Rodd the housekeeper dusting the dining-room table, and though servants must be kept in their place she felt an overpowering desire to speak of her problem to someone.

"Do you know," she said, "what Philip calls that rabbit of his now?"

"Nome."

"He calls it Shred—no, Sredni Vashtar. Have you any idea what he can mean by it?"

"I'm sure I couldn't say, 'm."

Mrs. van Beer looked at her disappointedly and then went out of the room. Mrs. Rodd said something unfriendly under her breath, but whether it was directed against Philip or her employer was not discoverable. Probably it was not against the boy, for when she went to the French window herself she spoke to him quite friendly.

"How's King Zog, Philly?" she said.

"His name's Sredni Vashtar now," replied the boy.

"Well! What a funny name."

Philip looked at the housekeeper as if he suspected a trap. He surveyed her silently for a few seconds and then only said:

"You can hold him if you like."

He took the rabbit out of its hutch and cuddled it possessively. He looked undeveloped for his age, and his voice was shrill. You would have thought him nine rather than eleven. In the glance which he fixed on his pet there was concentrated an intensity of affection which would have made an intelligent observer wonder if his mental development was any more normal than his physical. Even Mrs. Rodd, not a psychologist, doubted momentarily if it was good for the boy to be all that gone on the animal.

"Will he scratch me?" she said uneasily.

"Sredni Vashtar is fierce and savage," Philip informed her; "but he will not attack my friends."

Mrs. Rodd held him gingerly. Sredni did not look savage. His eye was mild and large, his pink nose twitched continually as if he was carrying on a tea-table conversation in sign language. He was fat and his coat was sleek. He turned his head and looked benevolently at Mrs. Rodd. He was a handsome rabbit, and you would say he was aware of it.

But other thoughts were in his head. His rabbity conscious-ness had realized that this new person was holding him loosely and timorously. With that terrific back-leg kick that rabbits can give he knocked Mrs. Rodd's arm back and shot into the air. As he landed he gave a thump of triumph with his hind leg, leapt forward again, did a sharp right turn while in the air, and ran off to the chrysanthemum bed, where he began to eat the heads off the young stems.

"Now!" said Mrs. Rodd reproachfully.

"You shouldn't have let him go," said Philip.

They both ran forward towards the rabbit who shifted farther into the bed.

"Rodd!" called Mrs. Rodd, sighting her husband the gardener. The three then settled down to the slow task of hemming the rabbit in.

From an upper window Mrs. van Beer watched. She was very, very angry. No animal can do so much harm to a garden as a rabbit. Sredni darted with unexpected speed up and down the garden. He would cover the whole length in a few seconds while the human beings charged desperately over the flower-beds after him. Rodd made some attempt to avoid damage, but Philip made none. And while he waited for them to catch up, the rabbit would eat the tops of a few plants. He never ate the lower leaves: the top appeared more succulent. Whether he knew or not that this destroyed any possibility of flowering is a question that it is no good asking a rabbit. He seemed indifferent, in any case; there are few things more equable than the expression of a rabbit nibbling the head off a prize bloom. He would let the hunters get within three feet of him and then leap off with his sudden half-turn in mid-air. It took them fifteen minutes to catch him, and the garden was heavily trampled as well as rather gnawed at the end.

Rodd immediately set to with a rake to undo some of the more obvious damage. Mrs. van Beer was not consoled by the sight. Did she pay him to clean up after rabbits, or as a gardener? She looked round in vain for someone to ask the question of. She felt how lonely she was.

2

ROSALIE VAN BEER COULD NOT HAVE ADMITTED TO HERSELF that she disliked her nephew Philip. He had bad habits which needed to be corrected, and because of his weak health a strict watch and control had to be kept on his amusements. To do this she spent her energies and time, as she saw it, devotedly. That she had any pleasure in thwarting him she never realized. At the most, she might have allowed that the thought that he was a thoroughly nasty child came rather too frequently to her mind. But the nearest she ever came to introspection was to reflect repeatedly on the dullness of her life, her lack of companionship, and the unfairness with which she was universally treated.

For this she had some excuse. She and her nephew Philip Arkwright were the last representatives of their family. She had no relatives whom she would recognize and in the corner of Devon in which she was practically condemned to live they had hardly any friends.

Philip's grandfather, Sir Henry Arkwright (knight, not baronet, without a title to pass on) had had three sons to inherit his considerable fortune. All three had served in the army during the war. Michael, the eldest, had been killed with thousands of others at Passchendaele. Arnold, the professional soldier, had been the only one to come through unscathed. He had served in the East, and after the war had gone with his young wife to take up a responsible post in East Africa. He had never been his father's favourite, but Sir Henry's letters had become kinder in tone after the death of his brother. Robert, the youngest, was called up in February, 1918. Before he went out, he married Rosalie Brentt, daughter of a tobacconist in the Wilton Road, Pimlico. It was a war-marriage like hundreds of others. Sir Henry was furious, but fathers' furies counted for very little in 1918. In any case, Robert never had time either to repent or to feel his wrath. He was posted as missing in July, 1918: he was never heard of again.

Sir Henry made the war-widow an allowance of £500 a year on condition she made no attempt to communicate with him. Rosalie had resented Sir Henry's rudeness at the time of her marriage; this deliberate insult was the first thing to embitter her. The allowance was paid regularly, even after she married an unpresentable dance band leader named Harry van Beer. Sir Henry was too indifferent to pay any attention. Robert was dead, and like all young men had made a fool of himself and left messes for other people to clear up. To him Rosalie was just a mess to be cleared up: Mr. Archibald Henderson of Simms, Simms, Henderson and Simms did not use those words to Rosalie but he made his client's attitude clear enough. Rosalie realized that for the family she was something the cat brought in.

When she was the only girl in the world, and Robert the only boy, she had had a rather common prettiness and a bloom. After Mr. van Beer married her she lost them. The firm little breasts became large bags, drawn up by a tight brassière so that she looked like a duchess or a pouter pigeon. The bottom and hips expanded; the chin doubled. Dye replaced the young sheen of the hair, lines came on the face, the nose grew beaky. Worst of all was the change of expression. The only girl in the world had had a cheerful, unclever face, made a little naïvely touching by a few unskilled

1918-ish efforts with paint and powder. Its chief expression was a simple determination to enjoy life. Mr. van Beer's suspicious wife had a bad-tempered, over-painted face. You could almost tell by the drawn mouth, and the deep lines from the nose to its corners, that she believed that she had been married for her money, and that it was true; that she believed her husband was consistently unfaithful to her, and that it was true; that she thought she was unpopular, unattractive and likely to get no more enjoyment out of life, and that it was true.

Harry van Beer ran a small car into a standard lamp on the Brighton road on a September night in 1927, and broke his neck. He was drunk, and the girl with him was not Rosalie. His widow did not put on mourning.

Rosalie took her ten pounds a week and her discontent back to Pimlico. The tobacconist's shop had long been closed. Pa was dead, and Mum lived in Dulwich with a married elder sister. They'd had words when Rosalie married and she had never made it up. They were common, and she belonged to a good family, even if she was done out of her rights. But Pimlico was sort of homely, and rightly considered it was almost Belgravia. It was true that Lupus Street where she had rooms couldn't be considered classy, really. Still the shops were gay and cheap: there was a very good Henekey's open there too. Port was a very ladylike drink; Rosalie began to spend quite a time there and pick up rather brassy-looking friends like herself, but older and more inclined to sponge.

It was the arrival of Arnold Arkwright and his wife and child early in the thirties which pulled her up when she was well on the road to becoming a middle-aged soak. Arnold had allowed his leave to accumulate, as wise colonial officers do, and had six months clear in which to settle his son's future school and have a long holiday in England. Curiosity or kindheartedness made Mrs. Arkwright write to Robert's widow. Rosalie gave up drinking in pubs, cleaned up her rooms, bought herself new clothes, and as long as the Arkwrights were in London behaved as ladylike as she could. She gushed over the child and chattered at her brother-in-law and sister-in-law, who found her rather boring and silly, but by no means the harpy and wanton that Sir Henry considered her. Perhaps they were kinder than they need have been, to make up for his rudeness. When they left Rosalie did not wholly return to her previous life: she kept herself *to* herself more.

The world would have said that was the salvation of her, but perhaps the world was wrong. It might have been better for Rosalie to continue on the alcoholic path. She was gradually losing her pride and suspicions, and acquiring a little geniality.

"'Lo, Rosy dear!"

Several ladies of uncertain, or but too certain, occupation had begun to greet her like that every morning and to suggest a little one at eleven. She was becoming more contented, and even learning to distinguish between the sugariest cheap Ruby and a drier, older port. She had begun to exchange confidences and had even listened without reproaches to one or two which showed the speaker was not all that a good girl should be. Port is not, it is true, good for the health when drunk steadily in large quantities, but she had a healthy and resistant body. She'd have been good for many years.

Now that was all changed. She didn't hear when she was called to across the road; she even refused offers of drinks, let alone buy a

friend one. She was called stuck-up, and she was; and she had nothing to compensate her for the loss of her friends. There is a peculiar
hell for snobs who cannot find fellow-snobs to practise snobbery
with: Mrs. van Beer sat for hours together in her renovated rooms
being genteel, despising the vulgarity of her neighbours, hating
her superior relatives, and being desolate in her heart.

She wrote regularly to Philip's parents in Africa, who long ago
wished they had never dug her out, and who answered irregularly.
She once went to call on Philip, who had been left in an English
boarding school. But the boy had taken a strong dislike to her
and the school very civilly asked her not to come again unless the
parents requested her to. Sir Henry was looking after his grandson
in England.

The end to this life came very suddenly.

Arnold Arkwright and his wife were due to come home on
leave. They were anxious to spend all the time they could with
their child and Sir Henry, so they telegraphed to him that they
would come by air.

He went down to Devon, to the small but luxurious house he
had built himself, where all the work was done by Rodd and his
wife, who had been his servants since 1919. The house was opened
up, beds aired, Arnold's favourite claret—Chateau Pontet Canet
1920—brought up with delicate care from town. Philip was excused
from school after a personal, pressing letter from Sir Henry.

The evening before they were due to arrive Sir Henry was sitting on a big wicker chair on the very lawn where the pet rabbit
later escaped from control. He was rather a heavy man, seventy-
five, and moved with difficulty. Once he was in a chair he disliked
having to rise again.

Rodd brought a telegram out to him. The sun was setting, but the light was strong enough for it to be read. Sir Henry fumbled with his glasses, at last put them on and read it. His face changed so suddenly that Rodd ventured to offer a remark without being addressed:

"Any bad news, sir?"

Not trusting himself to speak Sir Henry held the wire out for him to read. The aeroplane had crashed: the company regretted to report there were no survivors.

There was absolute silence.

After what seemed an immense time Rodd said hesitantly, "And Master Philip, sir. Shall I—"

"No," said Sir Henry in a harsh voice. "I must tell him myself." He tried to move from his chair and found it difficult. "Leave me for a while. I will come in later."

The clear sky grew a deeper blue, the few clouds began to lose their postcard-like pink colouring. In the long row of trees beyond the bottom of the garden the rooks cawed and rustled and at last settled down to silence. The trunks were black against a few last horizontal strips of orange sky. Still Sir Henry stared motionless towards where the sun had set.

The garden became dark, the lighter flowers standing out like white spots, and all colours were lost. Still the man in the chair, now an indistinguishable black humped figure, did not move. At last Mrs. Rodd said to her husband:

"It's not healthy for him, sitting out there in the cold night air, brooding. If you won't go and speak to him, I will."

Sir Henry didn't answer when she spoke to him, or move when she touched him. Nor would he ever speak or move again. His heart had stopped beating, without pain or shock. The doctor when he came said that it had been weak for a long time, and that there was no need for any inquest.

So it was that some days later Rosalie van Beer was summoned by Mr. Archibald Henderson to hear the reading of a will. Philip, a sallow, bronchial boy bearing marks of his birth in Africa, was there in a black suit, escorted by Mr. and Mrs. Rodd. Sir Henry's will left all his fortune, estimated at £78,000, jointly to Arnold and Margaret Arkwright, and if they predeceased him to their son Philip. Either of these legatees were to retain James and Elizabeth Rodd in their service, or if the Rodds chose to leave, a sum of £500 each was to be paid to them. No guardian was named for Philip, but Messrs. Simms, Simms, Henderson and Simms were named as trustees. The existing allowance paid to Mrs. van Beer was to be continued.

In the event of Philip's decease before the age of twenty-one, £2,000 each was willed to the Rodds, several bequests made to charity and the residue left to Mrs. van Beer. Sir Henry had not considered that eventuality very seriously, it appeared.

Rosalie after the reading of the will came up to Mr. Henderson.

"I am the poor boy's only remaining relative," she said. "I am his natural guardian. I expect you to recognize that."

Mr. Henderson looked at her uneasily. But there were no other persons with even a shadow of a claim.

"Very well," he said. "Very well. I suppose so."

Rosalie came down to Devon, occupied Sir Henry's house, and brought Philip back from school. She declared his health required a private tutor, and a young man selected rather at random from a scholastic agency bicycled in every day to educate him.

She called upon a number of Sir Henry's friends, who did not return the call, with the exception of the vicar. After a while he too spaced out his visits and forgot to invite her. She had not very much free money to devote to church objects; he permitted his natural dislike for her to have its head. She did not after all attend church regularly.

Only elderly Dr. Parkes, for whom her wholly imaginary illnesses and Philip's partly imaginary weakness were a considerable source of income, was continually assiduous. He would listen to her reminiscences for hours, rarely refused an invitation to stay to lunch, and was willing to be called out at any time of day or night. He wholly agreed with her opinion of Philip's weakliness and approved of nearly all of her prohibitions. The diet he prescribed for him corresponded exactly with her idea of a healthy diet for a child (the prunes-and-rice and plenty of sops system); for herself he insisted upon a good glass of good port after every meal and whenever she felt weak.

He was an old man, slight, with white hair and bowed head, and with a professional caressing voice. His practice had shrunk, and his bills to Mrs. van Beer were large and paid without question. He was not dishonest or in any way a dishonourable man. Later events threw an unkindly brilliant light upon him. But he was an averagely diligent G.P., with a professional equipment which had been moderately good in 1889, the last year in which he had attempted to learn anything, with failing eyesight and memory and with an increasing difficulty in concentrating. Lack of any other resources forced him to go on practising when he should have retired. He had to live, and for that reason someone else was to have to die.

3

F OUR MORE PERSONS MUST BE DESCRIBED TO COMPLETE THE picture. Edward Gillingham, Philip's tutor, was not present when the rabbit escaped. His visits were getting more and more infrequent, and this September there had been none at all, for Mrs. van Beer had decreed that Philip must have a holiday, because education was "overstraining him". Possibly this order was due to jealousy of Philip's admiration for him, for though Mr. Gillingham was not much interested in his sallow pupil, he was intelligent and patient, and was the only person in the world who spoke to the child as a reasonable being. But it was more immediately due to a circumstance that he never heard about. He had tutored Philip successfully for several months, and in May Mrs. van Beer had begun to telephone him and tell him to stay away, at first only for a day or two days, and then sometimes for a week at a time. As he was paid anyway, he did not trouble to inquire why. If he had suspected Mrs. van Beer was meditating dismissing him as soon as she could find a tutor nearer to her wishes, he might have been more inquisitive.

Mrs. van Beer believed in astrology; her second Sunday paper was purchased only because of its page "Advice from the Stars". Philip one day asked Mr. Gillingham about these predictions, and he, unsuspicious, told him the truth. Next Sunday when Rosalie commented in alarm over a prophecy of ill-luck next Tuesday owing to Saturn, Philip remarked:

"Mr. Gillingham says only silly old women believe that sort of nonsense."

"How dare you speak to me like that!" said Rosalie, flushing.

"Mr. Gillingham says the *Sunday* —— ought to be prosecuted for swindling. The planets don't—"

"You're talking about what you don't understand."

"The planets go round the sun," Philip informed her levelly, "and the earth's only a planet. They haven't anything to do with us and don't mind us a bit. Mr. Gillingham says only fools don't know that."

"I'll box your ears if you talk to me like that," shrilled his aunt. But she did not do so. She was afraid that if she struck Philip the Rodds would report her to Mr. Henderson, and she was by no means sure of her legal position.

For the Rodds, though servants by position and always correct in manner, were at least as well established in the house as she was. Under Sir Henry's will she could not dismiss them; and nothing gave her reason to believe that they were her friends.

Rodd was sixty-two, a taciturn, quick-moving dark man, who attended to the garden, the boots, the coals and so on as in Sir Henry's day. Mrs. Rodd was fifty-seven, grey, fat, and pleasant-featured, with a big hairy wart on her chin. They were to all appearances the typical "old retainers", devoted to the memory of the Old Master, affectionate to the Young Master, and resenting the vulgar intruder. A lawyer was later to paint that picture utterly convincingly to a jury.

But does the Old Retainer ever really exist? Most people who talk of him have never heard servants talk among themselves, or have any idea of what goes on when the green baize door closes and talk is really free in the servants' hall. The word "devotion", so common in romantic novels, is very rarely applicable to the sentiments there expressed: the "Family" would be surprised to learn with what coolness its interests are regarded. The Rodds, at least, regarded themselves merely as two persons, reasonably well-rewarded, who had performed very well a skilled task, one of whose conditions was a demeanour of respect and loyalty. Affection entered into it very little. Sir Henry they had become used to with the years. Rodd had considered him rather a testy old fool; Mrs. Rodd had considered him no more than she considered the black and white cat, whose death a week before had affected her emotionally on the whole rather more. Like the cat, he had always been about the house and she missed him, though his ways were definitely less endearing.

Philip they liked because they had no reason to dislike him, and ordinarily kind-hearted people will like a child unless it annoys them or causes a great deal of work. Mrs. van Beer they disliked because they considered she was really their own class and was putting on airs.

But all these emotions were really of small importance. They hardly deserve writing down at such length. In the heart of the Rodds, if you could have looked there, you would have found as chief interest the accumulation of enough money to retire to a cottage of their own. They had a bit put away, and they had more than once discussed asking for Sir Henry's £500 and leaving. But the job was an easy one, and they were saving money all the time; on each occasion they decided to hold on.

Mrs. Rodd did her work efficiently as in Sir Henry's day. Rodd took advantage of Mrs. van Beer's ignorance of gardening to do less and less. The ivy along the garden wall and the south side of the house was never clipped. The vegetable garden grew less productive. Though the lawn was rolled and mown, the flowerbeds were filled more and more with nasturtiums, michaelmas daisies and other flowers that take little of a gardener's time.

His life was in one particular way more comfortable than in Sir Henry's day, also because of Mrs. van Beer's ignorance. Sir Henry had kept a very good cellar, and on her second night in the house Mrs. van Beer had ordered Rodd to bring up a bottle of red wine. He brought up a sound Mouton d'Armailhacq, 1929.

"Peuh!" said Mrs. van Beer when she tasted it. "It's sour. Did Sir Henry drink this?"

"Yes, madam."

Rosalie left most of the bottle, and the next night tried a different one, with the same result. Port was her taste, and she had never accustomed herself to French wines. A sauternes or a sweet graves might have led her gently on, but Sir Henry had nothing like them in his cellar. Eventually she consulted Rodd, in whose head a plan was forming.

"Is all Sir Henry's wine thin and nasty like this?" she said.

"I'm afraid so, madam," he said. "Sir Henry was very conservative, and never would realize you can keep things too long." He looked at the rows of bottles—there were over fifty dozen—and shook his head sadly. "It's all gone, I'm afraid, madam. No use except maybe for cooking. Turned to vinegar, it has."

"Oh, no, surely," said Rosalie, remembering not to say "Ow now".

"Well, madam, there's the port and the brown sherry. Now I should think those would be very good still."

A bottle of each was brought out. Sir Henry had kept them only for guests, and they were merely of medium quality. But their taste smoothed out Rosalie's frown.

"Now that's what I call really nice," she said. "We'll keep this. And you'd better throw all that stuff away."

"Yes, madam. If I might make a suggestion, madam."

"Yes, Rodd." Rosalie was gracious: port's first effect is graciousness, and its second bad temper.

"We can get the grocer to allow a penny each on the bottles. He'd pick up a dozen every fortnight or so when he hasn't got much on the cart. I'll speak to him, if you like."

"Very good," she said, and thought no more about it, except to note with pleasure that nearly every fortnight a credit of 1s. for empties appeared on the grocer's book.

Meanwhile Rodd extended and completed his education in wine. Almost any evening an observer rude enough to stare in at the windows could have noticed the mistress of the house sitting in the big dining-room gobbling her dinner and rather shame-facedly drinking indifferent port in large gulps. In the kitchen the gardener and his wife slowly and thoughtfully would be eating a dinner in no way inferior, prefacing it with a glass of very unusually good dry Amontillado, and accompanying it with a bottle of—say—Steinberger 1929 for which any wine merchant would have offered them ten shillings on the label alone. Rodd drank two-thirds of a bottle every night, Mrs. Rodd the remaining third. Their digestions were noticeably, audibly even, better than their employer's. Rodd thought it wisest not to use the best glass, but took all wines in a claret glass; he educated his wife into smelling the bouquet of the wine, and serving it at the right temperature.

The fourth member of the household, Ada, had no part in this ceremonial, for she left each day at six. Her full name was Edith Ada Corney, and she bicycled over every morning from the nearby town of Wrackhampton, arriving at seven-thirty o'clock. She was an ugly girl of eighteen, daughter of a farm-labourer. She did all the rough work which Mrs. Rodd told her to do, spoke when she was spoken to, but not otherwise, and ate a very great deal of food at lunch—so much as to astonish Mrs. Rodd, who was herself a countrywoman. She had no noticeable fault except a tendency to eat any pieces of cooked meat, cold potatoes, or fruit which were incautiously left out in the kitchen. As with the majority of underfed and ill-housed country working girls, her face was pale and her teeth bad. She perspired very freely in the hot weather, and if she had any opinion concerning her employers she did not express it. She got 15s. a week and her gargantuan lunch, which was good pay for the district.

4

T WO DAYS LATER MRS. VAN BEER HAD HER PLAN READY.
In the morning she rang up Dr. Parkes and asked him if he
could manage to call about 12.30 and if he would be so kind as
to stay to lunch. Dr. Parkes found himself free to do so, and an
excellent lunch was provided.

The doctor sat down to it a little puzzled. He had been asked
to examine Philip before lunch and had been unable to find anything wrong. He had indeed begun to say so, as diplomatically as
he could, when Mrs. van Beer's attitude showed that this was a
most unpopular diagnosis. Even so all he could do was to sigh and
say, "Still a very nervous condition, I'm afraid. I think we must go
on with that tonic. I shall vary its composition slightly. Perhaps
you could send your man round for a fresh bottle this evening?"
He could not think that he had been sent for merely for this; but
when he inquired after Mrs. van Beer's health she quite unusually
declared herself to be feeling thoroughly well.

Conversation at lunch was on trivial topics, until with the
arrival of coffee, Rosalie said, "Now you can run and play in the
garden, Philip."

She turned to the doctor and said with a rather tigerish smile,
"I think we deserve a glass of port, don't you, Doctor?"

"Well, well: I won't say no." Dr. Parkes contrived to fill his
voice with archness.

She poured them each out a brimming glass. She put her
lips down to hers and drew up the wine into her mouth with

a loud suck. She did not believe in waste, as she was accustomed to say.

"I've been wondering," she said, "about Philip."

Dr. Parkes indicated attention.

"It seems to me so funny," she went on, "that in spite of all that you do for him—and I've *every* confidence in you, Doctor—he still doesn't get stronger. I'm wondering if there is any other reason." She hesitated and then leant across the table and said in a low penetrating voice, *"Have you ever thought of animals?"*

"Animals, dear lady?"

"Yes. Animals. The horridest diseases are carried by pets. Look at parrots, nasty things. People dying of that disease."

"Does Philip keep any pets then? Mice or rats? I didn't know."

"He kept some mice till recently which I had to have destroyed. They smelt very bad; I was sure it could not be good for him. And now he's got a very vicious rabbit, which he nurses and fondles all the time. He kisses its fur and I don't know what he doesn't breathe in. Of course its hutch is very nasty. You know what animals are. It seems to me all very insanitary. Don't you think that perhaps there might be an explanation in that, Doctor?"

Dr. Parkes folded up his napkin and looked judicial. "I think I ought to have a look at Brer Rabbit," he said, and began to rise, with a side glance at the decanter. Rosalie intercepted it.

"I think we deserve a teeny weeny bit more," she said, pouring out three-quarters of a glass each. For a couple of minutes they were silent, except for an involuntary noise from Rosalie. "Pardon," she said. "The heat of the day." Then they rose, and flushed and heavy walked out into the midday sun.

Philip was looking at the rabbit. He was down on his knees before the hutch and such an expression of adoration was on his face that you might have thought he was praying.

"Philip dear," his aunt flashed a toothpaste smile at him, "show Dr. Parkes your rabbit."

Philip looked at her suspiciously. There was nothing which she said to him that he did not think over twice, in order to find the trap in it. But he was proud of his rabbit and willing enough to show it off. He wrapped his arms round it and brought it to the doctor.

Dr. Parkes patted it. He saw a glossy-coated buck, mild-eyed and healthy, who appeared to be enjoying life. The buck suddenly stopped twitching its nose and laid its ears back. It also had seen something, but what it made of the doctor no one knows. It was probably only, as the lawyers used to say when opposing bail, *in meditatione fugae,* occupied in meditation of escape.

However, Dr. Parkes did not offer to take the rabbit, to Mrs. van Beer's disappointment.

"What's his name?" he said.

"Sredni Vashtar," said Philip, loudly and clearly.

"Eh? What? Well, well," said the doctor, a little startled. "And is this where his lordship lives? Let me have a look."

He bent down and looked at the hutch. It was not very clean, but it would have been a gross exaggeration to call it insanitary. And the rabbit was obviously in excellent health.

"I should say," he told Mrs. van Beer after they had left the boy, "that you need not be anxious about that animal. It appears to be in good condition. The hutch should be cleaned thoroughly as a precaution. But I doubt if it would carry any infection."

It was clear from her expression that Mrs. van Beer did not in the least want to cease being anxious.

"Well, of course you know best, Dr. Parkes," she said in a whining voice, "but I do feel surprised you should say that. He *fondles* that animal—pushes his face and mouth into its fur, all stinking with you know. I'm sure it *must* be harmful."

"Dear me, dear me; a very bad habit," said Dr. Parkes, trying to retrieve his mistake. "Philip!"

The boy sidled nearer.

"You must be very careful with that rabbit. Animals aren't clean, you know, my boy. You might catch something from it. Don't cuddle it. Don't ever put your face in its fur, or kiss it, or anything like that. Don't hold it any more than you must. Now remember. This is important. If you don't pay attention to what I say we might have to take the rabbit away."

Philip's face was distorted with a snarl of fear and hate. He bared his yellowish teeth like a dog, and then ran away without speaking. He saw all too clearly what was being plotted.

But Rosalie beamed. The necessary words had been said. She was certain that Philip would fondle the animal again. And then it would be "doctor's orders" to get rid of it.

5

M RS. VAN BEER DID NOT HAVE TO WAIT MANY DAYS. THE doctor had been to lunch on Tuesday, and on Friday she had her chance. It was her habit to dress her nephew in a yellowish Norfolk suit, with knickerbockers over his knee, such as nice little boys had worn when she was young. She went to great pains to get it, for even in rural Devon these are rare. She did not know how much he disliked it, and if she had it is not likely that it would have made any difference. It made the child very conspicuous: she could be sure of seeing him from her bedroom window wherever he might be in the garden. She spent a great deal of her time up in her bedroom watching over him (or spying, as you choose to phrase it). On Friday morning she saw him stealthily abstract the rabbit from its hutch and run with it in his arms down to the foot of the garden, where he was partly hidden by a rhododendron bush.

She came downstairs and went out into the garden, stepping as quietly as she could. She tiptoed towards the rhododendron and peeped through. She saw Philip clasping the rabbit closely to his chest, rubbing his nose into its fur, and reciting something in a slow singsong monotone. He was sitting on his heels and swinging slowly to and fro in rhythm with his hymn.

She watched him a moment and then burst through on him like a charging rhinoceros.

"Philip!" she shouted. "How dare you disregard the doctor's orders? He said if you did that again the rabbit would have to be killed. It's most unhealthy. Put it back in the cage at once. I'll see what's to be done about you later."

"It's not true," he cried shrilly. "He never said it. I'm doing nothing wrong."

"Put it back in the cage," she repeated.

Sullenly he dawdled back and put it in the hutch.

At lunch he could not eat his food. Perhaps he was sick with apprehension; anyway Mrs. van Beer drew a convenient moral. "You see, Philip, the doctor was right. He said that messing that nasty beast about made you ill."

"He didn't. He didn't. Auntie, *please* don't do anything to my rabbit."

Auntie said nothing.

After lunch she sent Philip up to lie down, to recover, as she said. She gave him twenty minutes and then went out as quietly as she could to the hutch. She was clumsy, or frightened: the rabbit nearly escaped, and there was an audible scuffle. He bit her again, and tore her wrist with a fierce kick from his back leg. But at last she captured him and took him into the kitchen, which was cleaned up and empty except for Ada, Mrs. Rodd being in the housekeeper's room, dozing after lunch.

"You can leave us, Ada," said Mrs. van Beer, using the plural presumably for self and rabbit.

"Ow," said Ada, and did so.

Mrs. van Beer dashed to the gas oven, thrust the rabbit inside, slammed its door and turned on the jets full, not light-ing them.

She stood still for a moment, quivering all over with a peculiar excitement. At that moment, Philip, all of whose suspicions had been aroused, ran down the stairs and opened the kitchen door.

"Auntie, what are you doing? Auntie, *where's my rabbit?*"

"Be quiet," she said angrily, "it's for your own good." She gave him a strong push in the chest and sent him reeling back into the passage. She shut the door and leant against it.

The rabbit was kicking and fighting in the oven. Perhaps it realized what was happening, for it gave that high scream of terror which rabbits only give under the fear of death. Philip beat sobbing on the kitchen door. Mrs. van Beer still stood against it, breathing very fast and clenching and unclenching her fists. Her excitement was increasing and her face was red.

The rabbit was now ceasing to struggle.

Philip's cries woke up the housekeeper. Mrs. Rodd ran up anxiously.

"Goodness me, boy, what is the matter?"

"My rabbit," wept Philip, even in this extremity having wit enough not to mention his aunt. "He's in there and I think he's dying."

"Gracious!" said Mrs. Rodd, and turning the door-handle pushed firmly forward. Mrs. van Beer was not in the least prepared for a firm adult shove and gave way.

"I *beg* your pardon, mum," said Mrs. Rodd as she walked in. "Heavens!" she added. "We'll all be blown up."

The room was reeking with gas. Mrs. Rodd rushed to the oven and turned it off. Philip opened the door: the rabbit was limp and its eyes were glazed.

"It had to be," said Mrs. van Beer a little uneasily.

Philip held the body of his pet for a moment in his arms. His face twisted, he looked as if he were going to burst into tears. Instead, he laid it down on the floor and stood up. On the kitchen table was a short tapering knife. He jumped forward and flung it with great force in his aunt's face, where it made a light cut on her left cheek.

"You beastly old woman," he screamed. "Swine! Swine! Swine!"

He threw himself at her, kicking and clawing, a whirling flail of childish anger. His thin legs and arms in his ridiculous Norfolk suit banged helplessly against the stout and heavy woman.

Rosalie's face was nearly as furious as his. She pushed him away and then deliberately, with all the strength she could, struck him a violent blow on the side of his head, sending him staggering across the room. Mrs. Rodd, with a shocked expression, put herself between them. Philip fell on the floor and Rosalie, as dignifiedly as she could, sailed out of the room.

Distress and the gas-ridden atmosphere had its natural effect on Philip. He was sick. He lay on the floor, his head pillowed on his dead pet, sobbing and retching alternately until Mrs. Rodd, with an expressionless face, gathered him up in her arms and took him up to his room.

Later in the evening Philip came down again. He found Rodd. "Where's my rabbit?" he said. Rodd looked at his drawn face and decided to answer truthfully.

"In the woodpile," he said. "I was going to bury him."

"Lend me your spade," said Philip.

Rodd nodded towards it.

Philip went down with it and with the body to his favourite playing place behind the rhododendron. There he dug a grave, and laid the rabbit within it. He did not place any headstone or mark upon it. He would always know where it was and he did not want his aunt to know. Tears were pouring down his face all the time, but he was not sobbing. He was muttering to himself continually; without ceasing; all the time.

6

O N MONDAY MORNING NEXT EDWARD GILLINGHAM LEAPT lightly off his bicycle and walked in by the front door. Mrs. van Beer was taken by surprise. She had forgotten that the tutor was due to resume his duties that day. If she had remembered, she would have put him off. Indeed, she began to go downstairs to say that Philip was ill; but it was too late. Philip had heard him come in and rushed to meet him, gripping him by the wrist fiercely and almost dragging him to the schoolroom. Edward was startled by this vehemence, and perhaps for the first time looked at his pupil closely.

He saw the eyes sunken in and red-edged, the sallow peaked face more sallow and peaked than ever, and a general expression of deep misery. His conscience rebuked him. He had never paid enough attention to the child. After all Philip was an intelligent boy, interested in his work and with a mind worth developing. It wasn't his fault if he was pert and given to fits of bad temper. Any one who had to live with that ghastly aunt would show traces of it. He must be kinder to him. He spoke to him as they sat down at the table, in a warmer tone than usual.

"It's very nice to see you again, Philip." He smiled at him as friendlily as he could.

The result startled him. Philip laid his head on his arms and burst into tears. His sobbing was not loud, but it was violent; his body shook with it. Edward rose in alarm and put his arm round his shoulders. "What is it, old man?" he said. "Tell me. Is there anything I can do?"

This evidence of affection, a thing so little known to Philip, had as its first effect to worsen the crisis, but in a few minutes he began to control himself. "She murdered him," was the first coherent sentence he got out; and then in due course brought out the whole story.

Edward wrote that evening about it to a young woman named Ellen Cartmell. (She was twenty-three to his twenty-four; to the world she was moderately pretty, with a snub nose, a wide mouth, a fresh complexion and rather thick ankles; to him she was unparallelly beautiful and lightened any room as soon as she came into it. That is to say, he was in love.)

"This morning (he said) I had a curious and unpleasant experience. You remember me telling you about Philip Arkwright, the boy whom I tutor and who lives with a very disagreeable aunt named van Beer? Well, before I could get down to work he suddenly started howling; and when he was able to talk he said the aunt was a murderer. She keeps him very much under her thumb—won't let him play with other children, and treats him as an invalid.

"It appears she quite wantonly killed his rabbit, the only thing he has to play with. There was hardly a shadow of an excuse and it sounds very malicious.

"I've never seen any one so heartbroken. I think the child is very unhappy and lonely, and he had given the animal all the love that he could find no other home for. I couldn't understand all he said, but in some way he seems to have believed that the rabbit was exceptionally wonderful, remarkable, and even powerful; it was a sort of fetish and he used to give it a sort of ritual, if that is the right phrase. Anyway, it died a very mean sort of death in a gas oven, and his whole world seems to have been overturned. There was a sort of horror as well as sorrow in the poor child's face.

"He talked very fast and confusedly, and kept asking me if murder would be punished. I did my best to comfort him, but I'm afraid I'm not very good at that sort of thing. We didn't do very much work, but he did calm down a little. I think I'm almost the only person he talks freely to.

"When we were finishing, this aunt of his came in. She's a middle-aged brassy woman, rather false genteel and I should think very selfish. She smiled toothily at us both when I stood up and said: 'Well, Philip dear, are you getting on nicely?' He didn't answer and I do hope that never, never in my life, any child, or anybody at all, looks at me as he looked at her. I've never seen such hatred. She looked pretty disagreeable too, I must say.

"So then she said, 'I should think you'd better stop; you mustn't work too hard, darling.' But this time she didn't look at him at all, but turned her head aside. I was going anyway, so it didn't matter her stopping us. But I didn't like the atmosphere at all, and I will try and take more care of that boy.

"Some day, my darling, we will have *lots* of children of our own. We'll be surrounded by them, all we can afford; and we will love them all, and the house shall be full of happiness. We'll let them sing and dance and shout, and keep rabbits and rats. And you will be there among them. After that dreadful house, there's no person I want and need to see more than you. You are loveliness, and cleanness, and kindness; and everything that that house isn't. Every time I think of you and remember what you are..."

The rest of the letter is nothing to do with anybody but the two of them.

7

As soon as she had disposed of the tutor, Mrs. van Beer went out into the garden. She stood on the red brick paving which ran the length of the house and looked round her. The place was far from tidy. The bed facing her was full of dead montbretias, which had not been cut down. Their browning leaves and leggy stalks were unsightly. A whole large spray of the unkempt ivy had fallen away from the house and swayed slowly in the breeze. Little streaks of ivy dust lay about the bricks, there were some unidentifiable leaves scattered around, and even a bunch of withered cut flowers, thrown down there and left to die. There was a bed of nasturtiums which was thick with black fly. Only the lawn was well kept.

Mrs. van Beer, if she saw any of this, said nothing. Her nephew came out of the house after her, and she looked at him with a curious expression. He stared back at her, as warily as a cat. In a few seconds they both went down the garden, separately.

An hour later they both sat down to dinner. On the table, waiting, was a cold leg of lamb and a salad consisting of lettuce, cucumber, and beetroot, dressed by Mrs. Rodd. The lamb was tasteless and the salad gritty, but they neither of them mentioned this. Indeed, they hardly spoke. Mrs. van Beer once said, "Eat your food up, Philip"; he did not answer, but did as he was told.

After lunch he went out and played in the garden: Rosalie stayed in to drink her usual glass of port. There was a third of the bottle left; she said aloud, though no one was listening, "It's hardly worth keeping," and refilled her glass until the bottle was finished. It was a very hot September day, and though the sun did not come into the dining-room, it was oppressive indoors. She was sleepy and flushed; her cheeks had a rather purplish colour.

About half-past three she entered Mrs. Rodd's room. She was dignified, but greenish yellow. "Mrs. Rodd," she said, "you must throw that meat and that salad away. There's something wrong with it. I felt very queer just now, and went to get a little bicarbonate. Before I could take it I came over very ill, and I've thrown up everything. *Everything*," she repeated with sombre satisfaction.

"Perhaps it was the port, madam, this hot weather," said Mrs. Rodd innocently.

"Certainly not," snapped Rosalie. "Throw that food away *at once*."

"Yes, madam," said Mrs. Rodd, and went to the kitchen to do so.

Later in the afternoon Philip came in and sat down in Mrs. Rodd's kitchen. He said nothing, but trembled as he sat. She looked at him and said, "Anything wrong, Philly?" As he did not answer she looked a second time at his white face. "You're all quaking," she said.

"Don't feel well," he said in extremely tired tones. "I'm all shaky. My head aches."

"I think I'll be sick," he added, brightening a little as a child does at the prospect of any unusual event. He went upstairs, Mrs. Rodd's eyes following him anxiously.

"Perhaps that meat wasn't all right after all," she said to Ada. "I'm glad the dustman calls to-morrow; I wouldn't like it smelling the place out."

Philip refused his tea, and went to bed at seven o'clock. His aunt suggested it and for once he agreed to something she said without any hesitation. She seemed wholly recovered and ate a large quantity of bacon, sausages, fried eggs and tomatoes, with a thick slice of fried bread, O.K. sauce and a tin of peas, followed by lemon blancmange and tinned pineapple; she drank more port with it. This she did with relish and apparent immunity.

In the morning Philip seemed worse. He got up to breakfast very unwillingly, ate a little porridge and threw it up immediately. He went to lie down, and his aunt—not failing to point the moral to Mrs. Rodd—took his temperature. It was 101; she gave him her universal remedy, syrup of figs.

He vomited it.

Rather later in the day (no one afterwards could remember the time), Mrs. van Beer rang up Dr. Parkes. "I think Philip has eaten something that disagreed with him. He's been sick and he's a little feverish. Could you manage to look in this afternoon?"

Booking another fee, Dr. Parkes agreed and arrived at a quarter past four. At the gate he met Edward Gillingham, who came in the afternoon on Tuesdays and Thursdays instead of the morning owing to another teaching engagement. They walked up the path together.

"I don't expect you'll be needed to-day, young man," said the doctor. "I hear our little friend has something wrong with his tummy."

"Oh. I'm sorry. I'll come in, though, and see."

They were both shown into the untidy sitting-room. Edward remained in the room while the doctor went upstairs.

Some people have nearly all the social virtues and retain just one childish fault. Edward was one of these. He was honest, polite, courageous, affectionate and intelligent. But he was inquisitive. He nosed into everybody's business; he could not help it. Several times he had been on the verge of discovery and a minor humiliation; even his Ellen had once had to tell him to mind his own business. He walked up and down the room, peering into the ornaments, looking at the calendar mottoes for nearly a week ahead, and picking up the books. In one of these he was surprised to find a cutting from the *East Essex Monitor* of a year ago. He opened it out and read it with absorbed attention. His mother had first commented when he was nine that he'd be rich if only he'd give to his work the same passionate interest that he gave to things that hadn't the least possible importance to him. This one turned out to be a report of an inquest. When he had read it, he refolded it and put it back, and looked for more fodder. He found a yellow-backed book which had belonged to Sir Henry and whose title was effaced. On the page which he opened he read the words:

"Oscar, you have been down the area again!"

Very much astonished, he sat down to read it, and made his first acquaintance with Whistler's correspondence. He did not move again until Dr. Parkes reappeared.

"You can't give your charge any lessons to-day, I'm afraid," he said. "The heat and some bad food have been too much for him."

"Is he seriously ill?" said Edward, as he walked to the gate with Dr. Parkes.

"Oh, I don't think so. No. No. A little bicarbonate in warm water, and a good rest will do wonders in a case like this, you know." Dr. Parkes climbed into his car and smiled amiably at this young man whose name he had forgotten—why was the fellow walking away instead of going back to the house? Oh, ah; he was the tutor, of course, not a relative. He put his car into gear and set off with a violent jerk and scrunch. The engine stopped almost at once, because he had left on the handbrake. "I forget so easily," he said to himself, and then stamped on the thought, for it was one he dared not allow.

Next morning he was summoned by an urgent telephone message from Mrs. Rodd, sounding very unlike Mrs. van Beer's cooing tones. Please to come at once, Philip was much worse. He did come at once.

He was escorted upstairs, and outside the door Mrs. van Beer spoke to him, with Mrs. Rodd listening on the stairs. "Philip has been sick continually, Doctor. He couldn't even keep down the bicarbonate you ordered; he said the other medicine hurts him and I haven't given it him this morning. He wouldn't have kept it down anyway. He looks *very* ill, and he's quite exhausted. And his last sick seemed to me to have blood in it."

Dr. Parkes said nothing, but the last sentence had made him start. His face grew more anxious when he saw Philip, who was still now and very hollow-eyed. He was sweating lightly and scratched himself half-unconsciously. Dr. Parkes tested his heart, and his anxiety suddenly doubled. Mrs. van Beer said: "What is it, Doctor? Is he worse?"

"Just leave me with him for a moment, alone, please," he replied gravely.

When she had gone he sat down by the bed but he did no more than look at the boy. He had come to a point which he had hoped never to reach. For there had happened to him the worst thing that can happen to a doctor. His patient was in grave danger, as he could see, and he realized that he had no idea whatever the cause could be. A younger man might know. But he, he was as much use as an African medicine man; and for all he knew he might have done nothing but harm up till now. The vomit did contain blood; he had seen that at once. That was an unmistakable warning; but of what?

He looked at the boy, who seemed nearly comatose, and made up his mind. He went out, shutting the door silently, and said:

"Mrs. van Beer, I'm afraid we ought to have a second opinion. The case presents some very baffling features. Unless you have any other suggestions I would like to call Dr. Herrington of Wrackhampton into consultation."

"Oh, Doctor, is Philip seriously ill?"

"I am a little worried," he admitted. "I think we should have this second opinion as soon as possible. I should like to telephone now if I may."

"Whatever you say, Doctor."

Dr. Parkes telephoned, and came back to say that he and Dr. Herrington would return at half-past twelve—earlier if possible.

The two men came in fact at a quarter past twelve. Dr. Herrington was a tall dark man of about forty, very alert; Dr. Parkes looked very dejected. Mrs. Rodd ran hastily towards them.

"Thank goodness you've come," she said. "It's been awful. He's been terrible. It's blood now, always." She followed them upstairs. "He won't have his auntie near him."

Philip had opened his eyes soon after Dr. Parkes had left and had seen Mrs. van Beer looking at him. Mrs. Rodd was standing by the door. He spoke in a faint voice but very distinctly, with long pauses.

"Go away. Don't ever come near me again…"

"Mrs. Rodd…"

"Don't let Auntie come near me."

Mrs. Rodd had come near the bed and said diplomatically, "It's all right. *I'll* be here."

"I want… Mr. Gillingham."

"He isn't here to-day, dear; you aren't strong enough for lessons."

"I want… to talk… to him."

"I'll tell him when he comes to-morrow, and if Doctor lets him, I'm *sure* he'll come up."

Philip had shut his eyes.

The two doctors went into the room, and both figures, the tall alert dark one and the bowed white-haired and shaking one, stopped short momentarily at what they saw. Then the first strode quickly to the bed. Dr. Parkes closed the door in Mrs. Rodd's face.

About ten minutes later he came out and asked for Mrs. van Beer.

"This is a great shock," he said a little incoherently. "I am sorry. Philip is—"

"He's dead!" cried out the woman.

The doctor bowed his head. "I think Dr. Herrington should speak to you."

The younger man had come up behind him, and intervened:

"I am very, very grieved. We did all we could for your nephew. But it was too late. And," he said with a slight sigh, "I feel I must tell you now that we are not satisfied of the cause of death. I am very loth to add to your distress, but Dr. Parkes and I have consulted and we feel there must be an autopsy."

Mrs. van Beer looked at him with wide eyes, and without a word ran into the dead boy's bedroom.

8

MOST OF THE WINDOWS OF THE CORONER'S COURTROOM were closed, from some obscure habit, though the day was hot and the room crowded. Dr. Saunders, the Coroner, continually wiped his forehead, but it never seemed to occur to him to order the room to be better ventilated. The air quickly became foul; heads ached and attention wandered.

Dr. Parkes was the first witness. He seemed to have aged greatly; his stoop was more marked and his face very lined and tired. He answered questions in a halting and unconvincing manner. He seemed frightened.

But dog does not eat dog; Dr. Saunders was very considerate to his fellow-practitioner. It was well known to all local doctors that Parkes was long past his work, but why humiliate the poor man? What was done couldn't be undone, and there was the prestige of the medical profession to be considered. Parkes was probably too old to do much more harm anyway.

Dr. Parkes gave a brief history of the case.

"When you were first called in, were there any symptoms out of the ordinary?"

"No, no; not at all."

"Was the boy subject to nervous indigestion?"

"Yes, very subject, very subject indeed; I was called in for that reason more often than any other. In fact he seemed much more a nervous child than an ailing child."

Dr. Parkes was recovering a little of his poise. He stated that he had at first actually only prescribed bicarbonate, and a common indigestion mixture. This he had done because the boy's condition had always yielded to those remedies before. He had made inquiries and found that some mutton which the child and his aunt had had at lunch was thought to be tainted. The aunt also had been sick. There was no symptom of any kind which would have led to any other diagnosis than his own.

The coroner made no comment, and Dr. Parkes suddenly drooped in the witness box again. Perhaps his little spurt of self-assertion had been unwise; after all the boy was dead and he was by no means sure even yet that it was not his fault. But how could any one have anticipated anything so extraordinary?

He more subduedly continued his account, stressing particularly the bleeding on the second day and the weakened pulse. The boy had a weak chest (the coroner raised his eyebrows at this colloquial phrase) and no doubt that had impaired his resistance. He offered the opinion, which did not seem to be going to be volunteered from any other quarter, that nothing more could have been done for him.

Dr. Herrington had but little to add. He had been called in very late to the case. The case was a very perplexing one. The suspect food had been thrown away, but the vomit had been kept. He repeated some of Dr. Parkes's remarks in more technical terms.

The foreman of the jury began to nod. Time passed and suddenly he found himself letting out an enormous yawn. He pulled himself together just too late; the eye of the coroner was fixed upon him and he turned scarlet with shame. He endeavoured to fix his attention upon the evidence now being given, which was that of Dr. Lammas, Acting Pathologist to the County. He had some excuse for his lassitude, for Dr. Lammas had quite unnecessarily repeated the effect of the evidence given already by Dr. Parkes, on the excuse of stating the information that he had been given before commencing his investigation.

The coroner was saying, "You then conducted a post-mortem of certain organs from the body of the deceased?"

"I did."

"Perhaps you will tell the jury in non-technical language what you discovered."

"Using non-technical language," said Dr. Lammas blandly, "I may say I found nothing at all." He seemed about to stop there and the coroner made a disapproving noise.

"I mean by that that I found nothing which the symptoms detailed to me by Dr. Parkes did not lead me to expect. There was inflammation, as might be expected. There were clear signs of extensive internal haemorrhage. But there was no trace of any substance which might have caused this condition. There was evidence of bronchial pneumonia in an early stage. It would not have caused the symptoms described.

"I therefore proceeded, with the assistance of Mr. Herbert Wilkins, the Public Analyst for the County, who is in court, to an analysis of the vomit which had been preserved. Here I found, as I had begun to expect, clear traces of poison."

At this word there was a sharp stir in court, and even the foreman sat up.

"Of what poison, Dr. Lammas?" said the coroner.

"Of hederin."

"What?" said the foreman of the jury, somewhat inelegantly.

"Hederin," said Dr. Lammas coldly. "Its formula is $C_{64} H_{104} O_{19}$. It is a glucoside, not an alkaloid as you might think. Perhaps it might assist you if I were to describe this as a case of ivy poisoning."

The foreman was sharply taken aback. There was a rustle in court and some whispering. One juror distinctly said "Coo!" The coroner frowned and continued:

"Is this form of poisoning common, Dr. Lammas?"

"It is exceedingly rare. Serious prior cases hardly seem to exist, but there are examples of mild poisoning. The substance has a marked purgative and emetic effect, and produces a rash and itching, the latter of which the deceased suffered from, though the first is not recorded. It produces extensive haemorrhage."

"You found sufficient to indicate that hederin glucoside was the cause of death?"

"I did."

The foreman had now recovered, and was anxious to show his alertness.

"Can the doctor explain, if this was what killed the poor child, how it is there was no trace of it in the body?"

"No doubt the vomiting is a sufficient explanation of that." Dr. Lammas was curt.

"'ow—*how* could he have got it?"

"That is not for me to say."

"I think the police have some further evidence on that point," said the coroner hastily, and dismissed Dr. Lammas before the foreman could intervene again.

Sergeant William Arthur Knowles deposed that he had inspected the house where deceased had lived. He had been instructed to pay special attention to any ivy that might be there. He found the ivy at the back of the house very overgrown and much of it very loose. There was ivy pollen all over the place in a manner of speaking. There was an especial lot of it on the paving immediately outside the dining-room.

"Did you form any idea of any way by which the boy could have consumed the ivy pollen?"

"Very hard to say, sir. It couldn't have blown in, and it's hardly likely he would deliberately have eaten enough to poison him. I understand that would be quite a noticeable amount. But without going so far as to make a definite statement, I can say I was informed that both he and Mrs. van Beer, his aunt, were taken ill after lunch, Mrs. van Beer fortunately recovering. Now I have ascertained that for lunch they partook of a green salad from the garden. It has occurred to me that perhaps this salad may have had ivy dust on it, and—"

A loud and very angry voice interrupted him from the body of the hall.

"That's a lie, Mr. Knowles; how dare you say such things about me?"

"Who is that woman?" said the coroner, rising in wrath.

An angry housekeeper stood up. "My name's Elizabeth Rodd, and I demand to be heard."

"You shall be heard, madam. Till then be silent, or you will be turned out of court. Proceed, Sergeant."

The sergeant indicated that he had no more to say. The coroner overlooked what sounded like the word "Impudence!" from Mrs. Rodd, and summoned her to come forward.

She controlled herself with difficulty.

"I never heard such a thing," she said in reply to the coroner's request to give her evidence. "My kitchen's spotless. Never in my life have I served a salad dirty. Let alone that the lettuce comes from the other end of the garden, where there's not a trace of ivy. I washed that salad carefully, every leaf of it. And I cut it up and I made the dressing; as carefully as I always have done. And there's those can bear me out. Ada! Ada! Now speak up." She jabbed her finger at the kitchenmaid who was sitting next to her vacant chair.

"Do I understand that you wish this young woman to give evidence?" said the coroner, trying to catch up with her.

"Did you or did you not see me wash that salad?" said Mrs. Rodd to her young assistant, who had stood up in the body of the court.

"Indeed you did so, 'm; very carefully, and showed me how to do it and how to make a dressing. Not a doubt, 'm."

Mrs. Rodd breathed through her nose and glared at the sergeant, who looked deprecating.

The coroner in his summing up said that it was uncertain how the boy had absorbed the hederin poison, but that need not affect the verdict. It was a question that might remain for ever unsolved. Boys did the oddest things. A few further generalities, and he closed.

The jury returned a verdict of "accidental death".

Two days later Edward Gillingham read the report in the local *Argus and Courier*. He folded the paper up and put it down disconsolately. A highly important and personal problem faced him.

9

I F HE SAID NOTHING WHATEVER, THERE MIGHT BE A MISCAR-riage of justice. There might be; it was not certain.

But if he spoke, it was very certain that things would be uncomfortable for him. In the first place he would have to expose himself as a Nosey Parker. In the second, he would have in effect to bring against someone the gravest possible accusation that can be made. For unless his item of information meant a charge of murder, it meant nothing at all. And on top of all that, it was quite possible that after having humiliated himself and having made this sensational accusation, he would be told there was nothing whatever to it.

Maybe there *was* nothing to it.

But once he had decided to believe that, the item of information would not stay quiet in his mind. It was an odd thing. No doubt of it. And the more he tried to push it aside, the more its oddness worried him. In the end he decided to do what any normal man does in a crisis—ask a woman.

Ellen listened to him carefully, her rather large fair face looking affectionately maternal, and her blue eyes steadily fixed on him. Before he had finished he knew what he would do, and what she would say. But he went on:

"…so while I was waiting for Dr. Parkes to come down—because he didn't think Philip was ill at all, and I might be going to give him lessons—I took up some of the books, which didn't seem to be much read anyway, and looked inside them. And in one of them I found a big newspaper cutting." He paused.

Ellen said, to start him off again, "Had it been there long?"

"Goodness, how do I know? Yes, I do, though. What an odd thing to ask. It must have been there some time, because its folds had made a mark on the pages on each side. Still I don't see what that means. Why?"

"Oh, I don't know. But what was it, anyway?"

"Well, it's not easy to explain what it means. I want you to look at this report in this week's paper again. Tell me what strikes you most about it. About the manner of Philip's death, I mean."

"I don't quite know what you mean." Ellen frowned in an effort to help. "Let me see. Well, he was killed by a vegetable poison that could be picked up in the garden. No one has any idea how he got it, though; and it seems odd that it should be an accident. But it must be an accident, because—"

"Because what?"

"Why, because nobody knew that this stuff could be poisonous. So no one could have done it on purpose. Even the doctors didn't know, and the famous specialist said there were practically no instances of it."

"That's the trouble. Somebody *did* know, and somebody had taken the trouble to cut out the information, giving an idea of quantities and the time of year and everything. I think this cutting must be one of the very few instances that the doctor spoke of. It came from a local East Essex paper of a year ago—not the sort of thing that you expect to find bought or kept by accident. It was an account of an inquest on a little girl of eleven. And she died of poisoning from ivy dust.

"The whole story was there, and it was just like poor Philip's. All the symptoms, just the same. Only in this case it was known how the child got hold of it, and it was a real accident."

"Oh." Ellen looked a little white but said nothing more.

Edward went on:

"So you see, somebody knew exactly what was happening. And somebody didn't say a word. Just let old Parkes bumble along. And, you see, nobody knows how Philip could have eaten the stuff by accident. It doesn't seem easy. The dining-room table's far too far away for it to have blown in, or anything like that. But somebody could have *given* it him. And somebody had kept that cutting for a very long time, for some purpose or other."

"Why should any one have wanted to kill poor Philip?"

"I don't know." Edward spread his hands out. "I believe there's money in the family."

Ellen looked very depressed.

"How beastly for you," she said. "But of course you'll have to tell." She hesitated a moment, and observing that he looked very disconsolate, added: "Would you like me to come with you?"

He would have, very much; but the suggestion was too much for his dignity. "No, indeed," he said. "Gracious me, I don't want my hand held. But I wonder what I should do? I can't just stop a copper and say 'Oy!' Ought I to go into Exeter and find the lord lieutenant or somebody?"

"Not the lord lieutenant, fathead; the chief constable. I'd go to the nearest town, which is Wrackhampton, and find the chief there. Or else there's Sergeant Knowles… He was at the inquest. Why not go and see him?"

So it was decided. But Sergeant Knowles heard only a few sentences before deciding that someone higher up than he must deal with it. He took Edward Gillingham with him to see the Chief Constable in Wrackhampton, Mr. Cooper Wills, who was not a retired military man, did not have a red face and brusque manners, and was not a fool. He had entered the police force thirty-five years before, intending to make it his profession; he had risen steadily and been appointed to his present position by a committee which was influenced by two ideas which it did not know were obsolete. It thought that a trained policeman should direct a police force, and that able public servants should be encouraged by promotion within the service. Mr. Cooper Wills had with him Inspector Holly, who was his probable successor; they both received Gillingham with cordiality. They did not hint at any surprise at his inquisitiveness and congratulated him on his public spirit. Within thirty seconds he was completely at his ease.

They asked him only one question worth noting:

"Do you think you could identify the book in which you saw that cutting, Mr. Gillingham?"

"I think I could. I'm not absolutely sure. It was a large blue book with a title like *Rambles in Old World Devonshire*; and I know what part of the shelves it was on. If I were to go there again I could probably find it."

"Thank you. You've been very helpful, Mr. Gillingham. I'll have to consider this very carefully. I may have to get in touch with you again, but I know where to find you."

Mr. Cooper Wills held out his hand.

10

"WELL?" SAID MR. COOPER WILLS, LOOKING AT HIS inspector. "Do we believe the young man?"

The inspector, iron-grey-haired and over fifty, crossed long thin legs and whistled noiselessly.

"I think so, sir. No reason for him to make up such a peculiar story. And very few people know about that case. I didn't till Dr. Lammas told me of it. I'm afraid he saw that cutting all right. He was quite willing to point out to us where it was, too. I expect it's there. Or was."

"Then, if so, what does it mean? Just a co-incidence?"

"Not the sort of coincidence I like, sir."

"No. But we've got a long way to go. We've got first to check up on his story. It's quite easy for the sergeant to go there and make some inquiries, and take an opportunity to look for it. The death is still rather mysterious, by any account, and there would be nothing out of the way in our telling Mrs. van Beer that we felt we ought to look into it further. But it's not so easy for him to take Gillingham along. Anyhow, we'll have to arrange something. But suppose we do, and suppose Sergeant Knowles finds it there? Where are we then?"

The inspector shook his head. "Not much farther on," he said.

Mr. Cooper Wills pursued the matter. "We're faced with the same difficulty as before. We have no idea whatever of how the poison can have been administered, first of all. The child seems to have eaten nothing except at lunch. Bad meat doesn't give you hederin poisoning, and the salad was all right. So, even if we prove someone knew ivy dust would poison the child; and that someone kept that information in a handy form, I don't know what we can do about it."

Sergeant Knowles made a noise, and indicated a desire to be heard.

"Speak up, Knowles: we can do with help if you've got any."

"Well, sir. I've been thinking that isn't quite so. There was time and opportunity for doctoring the salad. It was a cold lunch, and when I was examining Mrs. Rodd—the housekeeper, that is—in the course of my duties I elicited from her the information that the lunch had been laid and waiting a full half-hour before they sat down to it. Any one could have interfered with it. Now Ada, the skivvy, said to a young lady that I know" (the sergeant looked austerely impersonal) "after the inquest that Mrs. Rodd spoke out of turn in the witness box, and that she—Ada, I mean—thought the dressing was none too clean when she came to throw it away. But it was no good contradicting Mrs. Rodd when she was in one of her moods; better to say what she wanted you to quickly and be done with it. Also she added that she'd seen Mrs. Rodd wash it, so maybe she was mistaken."

"Not a very strong witness. But I think there's something there. Did Ada say what the salad dressing was like?"

"Gritty like, she said. As if there was dirt in it."

"Dirt. In fact, almost certainly ivy dust."

"If there was ivy dust in it, it was put there," said Inspector Holly. "Mrs. Rodd made it clear that it couldn't have come accidentally on the lettuces. They grow in a different part of the garden. Besides, she was seen to wash them."

"Ye-es," said the chief constable. "It looks like something. Then, if any one did it, who was it? Who had a motive? *Is fecit cui prodest.*"

"Pardon?" said the sergeant.

"I don't think there's any woman in the case," said the inspector, equally puzzled.

"Sorry. I meant, who profited by it?"

"Oh. That's not difficult, sir. Old Sir Henry's will is pretty well known. There are several legacies to hospitals—they're out of it. Mrs. van Beer gets the bulk of the estate if Philip dies before she does. Rodd and his wife get two thousand pounds each."

"Two thousand! That's a fortune for them."

"Mrs. Rodd threw away the salad," observed Inspector Holly. "She was very anxious to impress on the court that the salad was perfectly clean. She practically compelled Ada to support her in that, and there is good reason to believe it was a lie."

"Would she have kept this cutting? If she had, would she have hidden it in a book in the sitting-room? That's a good place to hide a paper, especially if the book is one not likely to be read. But it's hardly the place that Mrs. Rodd would put it. A book in the kitchen, or her bedroom—yes."

"It's not necessarily *hid* there at all, sir. I mean that whoever put it there may have done so temporarily, for one reason or another, and then mislaid it. Suppose he or she was reading it and someone else came into the room. Then he shuts it quickly up in the book, and puts it away. And there it stays. It's a good place to hide things, it's true; but you can hide things from yourself that way too."

"Even so, I don't see Mrs. Rodd using that room. What do you say, Sergeant?"

Sergeant Knowles started. "Well, for myself, sir, I'd like to know more about Mrs. van Beer."

"Go on."

"It looks to me this way. She didn't like the kid. Mr. Gillingham could tell us more about that, I believe; but anyway it's pretty common knowledge. They had a terrible quarrel about her killing a rabbit of his, and if half what Ada Corney has said is true, she's as malicious as they make them. It's true Mrs. Rodd threw away the salad, but who made her do it? Mrs. van Beer. Told her twice, Ada said."

"Ada seems to have a lot to say, Sergeant; I think she'd better say it to us. But remember, Mrs. van Beer was poisoned herself."

"Only slightly, sir. And this here cutting would tell her that it was a fairly safe risk to take, as the poison was only likely to kill a child. As a matter of fact, she didn't take hardly any risk. She was sick almost at once. She drank almost half a bottle of port at lunch and that did the trick. At least, it may have done. Or she may just have gone upstairs and put her finger down her throat."

"I see. Then you think she picked up a handful of ivy dust and mixed it in with the salad dressing in the half-hour while the food was waiting on the table. Maybe. It's possible. But we want more evidence."

"Yes, sir."

"There's just a chance somebody saw her. Concentrate on Ada, Inspector: she seems to know everything. Send the sergeant down there. See if she can remember—see if any one can remember seeing any one in the dining-room between the time when Mrs. Rodd set the table and they sat down. Let him have a quick look round for the book with the cutting in it and if he can't find it we must bring Gillingham in some way. Another thing. Find out from Wyman's at Wrackhampton and all the smaller newsagents who supplied anybody here with a copy of the *East Essex Monitor* a year ago. They are almost certain to have a record of it: it's not at all a common thing for someone in Devon to want an East Essex local paper. If none of them have a note of it, it means she probably ordered it direct. We can get an inquiry made at the offices of the paper in that case; they may have kept a record."

"Yes, sir." The inspector got up. Then he added: "There's someone else, besides those two women, who might have done it."

"You mean Rodd. Yes, I haven't forgotten him. He stands to gain by the boy's death too. He is as much under suspicion as Mrs. Rodd. But he had no access to the dining-room. On the other hand he might well have known, as a gardener, of the lethal effects of ivy. Quite a lot of what passes in textbooks for rare knowledge is common enough among country people, if only the London scientists knew. We certainly have to bear him in mind too."

"I didn't mean Rodd, sir. I meant Philip Arkwright."

"The dead boy? How on earth?"

"He may have determined to kill his aunt. She had killed his rabbit, you know; he detested her and he was a neurotic and passionate child. He may have got hold of that cutting and acted on the information in it. He could have mixed in the ivy dust in the salad bowl. It was ill-luck, from his point of view, that his aunt threw up her lunch, through boozing too much, while the amount he had to take himself to avoid suspicion turned out to be enough to kill him. He didn't realize he wasn't strong, perhaps."

"But if he read that cutting he must have realized he was almost certainly committing suicide."

"Maybe he did. Maybe he didn't care, so long as darling auntie died."

P ART OF A FURTHER LETTER FROM EDWARD GILLINGHAM TO
Ellen Cartmell, a few days later, after extensive inquiries
among the servants by the police, of which he did not know:

"…The business about poor Philip Arkwright is turning out badly.
This morning Sergeant Knowles called upon me and officially
asked me to accompany him to Mrs. van Beer's house. He had
with him a tall man who was introduced to me as Inspector Holly
when I saw them all at Wrackhampton. My job was to find that
cutting, but I wasn't contented with being told that. I know you
say I'm too curious, but after all I was a very important witness
and I was obliging them in a very essential matter, so it seemed
to me only fair I should be told something about it. So I asked
all the questions I could; they weren't in the least talkative but I
made it very difficult for them to say nothing at all.

"They wouldn't admit that they had definite suspicions, but
they did say that they had traced the order for the Essex paper
last year. It was given to the little newsagent near the Red Lion,
across the way from Wrackhampton Station. He generally sup-
plies Mrs. van Beer. He didn't remember the transaction at all
at first and only found it out by looking up his records. It was
an unusual request and the paper had to be ordered specially. At
first he said he didn't remember how it was ordered. Then he
said that it was ordered in writing by Mrs. van Beer. Then his
wife said that Rodd came in and gave the order verbally, reading

it off a slip of paper. Then she said: No, her husband was right. Inspector Holly thought that neither of them had the least idea and were just trying to oblige.

"I couldn't get anything more out of them. I wondered how they were going to explain my presence with them. They got out of that by offering no explanation at all. All the same, I felt very uncomfortable.

"The door was opened to us by Mrs. Rodd. The inspector asked where Mrs. van Beer was: she was down the garden. The inspector said he would like to speak to her, but might he ask Ada a question on the way? He assumed an invitation to enter, marched into the sitting-room, and left the sergeant and me there while he went through to the kitchen.

"Well, I recognized the book at once. I went to it, opened it and found the cutting there just as before. The sergeant inspected it and asked me if I was prepared to swear it was the identical cutting, in the same place as before, and that I saw it there the day before Philip died. I said I would state that on oath whenever it was required.

"We had to wait rather a long time then. The sergeant got rather fidgety. I heard afterwards that it wasn't Ada who was responsible for the delay. I don't know what she was asked or what she answered: they wouldn't tell me. But Mrs. Rodd had seemed very far from pleased to see us, and it was clear why as soon as the inspector got into the kitchen. Rodd was drunk. He was sitting in front of a bottle of burgundy which he had drank nearly all of. It seems that it came out of Sir Henry's cellar and the inspector thinks he has probably been robbing the stock fairly steadily. He spoke to him sharply, and Rodd told him to go to hell. They had 'words', and that took time.

"Well, in time the inspector came back into the room with Mrs. van Beer. The sergeant nodded to him, and he brought the woman forward face to face with the open book.

"'I should be glad,' he said, 'to hear what you have to say concerning this cutting, which has been found in this book in your drawing-room.'

"She bent over it. I couldn't see her face. While she was hesitating, he continued by reciting the usual formula—you know, warning her that whatever she said would be taken down and used as evidence.

"She gave a sudden sort of cry, a noise like *ang!* as near as I can write it down and her hands leapt forward at it. I think she would have torn it up if the sergeant hadn't caught her wrists.

"Then she began to shout. 'You can't do that. You're framing me! I don't know anything about it. You put it there yourselves.' She struck the sergeant across the face. I think she called him a damn lying swine. He hadn't spoken.

"I think she's a cruel woman and if she did kill Philip she deserves no pity. But it's not a nice sight to see even the worst human being arrested for murder. She sobbed and screamed, and kept appealing to them. 'Oh, let me alone! Can't you see I'm ill?' Her face was all yellowy and her hair came partly down. You could see she dyes it. Her face seemed suddenly to come all over lines. The inspector kept saying quietly 'I'm afraid I must ask you to come with me, madam', but in the end they had almost to carry her to the car. I think they didn't formally charge her till they got her to the station. I was left to walk home.

"I've been asking myself ever since what I thought of her behaviour. Did she seem guilty, or only frightened? I really don't know. I suppose the real question is: Did she have time enough to see what that cutting was about? Because if she did, then I suppose if she was quick enough to understand it, she would realize what might be made of it even if she was innocent. And then it would be perfectly natural for her to throw a sort of fit. But if she didn't, but knew all along what it was, then it looks pretty black. For it means that as soon as she saw they'd found it she knew the game was up.

"I can't answer that question, though I've thought it over time and again. I think the answer is that she may just have had time to grasp its meaning. In fact, no one can tell.

"All the same, darling, to-day I've done something that may mean hanging somebody. I don't feel happy. That's a very silly thing to say, I feel much worse than that. I am going to bicycle in and wait for you after your work to-morrow, and even if you do have to go to Princes Street I can go down with you. I don't want to be alone with myself, and after I've talked to you I'm not alone any more for the rest of the day."

M R. ARCHIBALD HENDERSON, WHO VERY MUCH DISLIKED
his position as Mrs. van Beer's solicitor, nevertheless had
decided that he owed it to the family to do his best to rescue
her. He had considered referring her appeal to some other firm
more accustomed to dealing with criminal cases, and had decided
against it. So he went to Sir Isambard Burns's rooms in King's
Bench Walk some mornings later, though with a heavy heart.
Although he repressed the thought as best he could, he was by
no means sure that his client was innocent. Sir Isambard was
altogether too cynical, and wholly disregarded the reticences
which a family solicitor likes to be observed. Besides, though
he had known him many years and called him his friend, Mr.
Henderson thought he was a climber, and the evidences of his
ambition which decorated his conversation were annoying. Finally,
Sir Isambard had decided to drive down to Devon that morning
to interview Mrs. van Beer in Exeter gaol, thereby disturbing all
Mr. Henderson's arrangements and ensuring him an attack of
indigestion. Mr. Henderson would much have preferred to travel
by train, getting there faster and not being incommoded by the
smell of petrol. But Sir Isambard had indicated that he needed
to consult him at length before the interview, and that the long
journey down in the big Packard would serve best for that. There
seemed no valid excuse for refusing. Sir Isambard was at the top
of his profession, and Mrs. van Beer would need all the help she
could get.

Sir Isambard was a thin, tall, very dark man with a face like a vulture and a monocle which he used only for conversational purposes. He was playacting most of his life, and some of the shows he put on brought him a lot of money. What were his real thoughts on any subject hardly any one knew, for he was unmarried. A rather stubborn and set solicitor like Archibald Henderson drew out his strongest tendencies to perverseness.

He had brought the elderly lawyer there at the unreasonable hour of ten o'clock, for an early start, and now that he had arrived would not give the signal for a move, even though Henderson fidgeted and more than once said, "Oughtn't we to be going?"

He persisted in talking politics, which his colleague disliked. He selected his distinguished rival Sir Stafford Cripps for examination, and reviewed his career since he was expelled from the Labour Party. (Sir Isambard, with well-managed publicity, had joined the same party a month before.) He considered the propaganda for a Popular Front and declared it doomed to failure. (This was before the Labour Party Conference had convinced Sir Stafford of the same thing.) Nevertheless, he said, he was glad of Sir Stafford's action.

"Glad?" said Mr. Henderson. "I should have thought you would approve of your Party's official policy at least for the first year of your membership."

Sir Isambard laughed, or rather cackled.

"I didn't say I didn't, my dear fellow. I only said this plays my game. Don't you see, the next Labour Government will have to give me a big job now. Before this, the two plums were settled already. Attorney General and Solicitor General, Sir Stafford Cripps and Mr. Pritt. Now it'll have to be Mr. Pritt and Sir. I. Burns."

Mr. Henderson coldly mentioned two other lawyers in the Party. Sir Isambard waved them away. He also refused the Lord Chancellorship in passing.

"You're not even in parliament yet," said Mr. Henderson irritatedly.

"Oh, *that*! I can be in as soon as I please. Simply a matter of choosing your constituency, spending money wisely, and taking meetings steadily. I speak everywhere that I have a chance now. I go down very well too, I can tell you. Don't you worry, it's all in the bag."

Mr. Henderson was a strong Conservative and this conversation was rapidly exhausting his patience. Exasperation so moved him that he forgot all his professional politeness and even resurrected from his memory a forgotten nickname.

"I really wonder, Ikey, if you can be as shameless as you pretend. One thing alone consoles me—this sort of talk will make it sure you never are offered any such post at all. And in any case the country will never let your people back into power again." He snorted and added, "I suggest we start out now."

Sir Isambard gave a loud, coarse laugh, and slapped him on the back. "I thought I'd get a rise out of you in the end," he said. "Come along then, and tell me why you distrust your client so much."

"Buffoon," said Mr. Henderson under his breath.

Aloud he said, as he climbed into the car, "I would not say I *distrusted* her exactly. It would be more exact to say I have little liking for her, and my reasons for that may not be wholly creditable to me. I—er, well, I find her very common. She was a shopgirl of some kind, I think, who married the youngest Arkwright brother during the war. He was killed, you know, and though old Sir Henry paid her an allowance he would never have anything to do with her. It was a mésalliance. Without doubt. She was a vulgar and silly woman, and for years she drank heavily. She married a dance band player for a while, which is where she got her name van Beer. He is dead. She has always seemed to me a greedy and jealous creature. If this unfortunate boy's parents had not died suddenly, she would never have been in the house at all. But as it was she claimed to be his natural guardian, and there seemed no plausible way of resisting the claim. I have reproached myself since, but I do not see what I could have done. She had given up drinking to any objectionable extent and her manner of life was unexceptionable. One cannot tell a court that one dislikes a woman's voice and manners." Mr. Henderson shook his head, and then went on to a general outline of the case.

Sir Isambard listened attentively. At the end he said:

"I take it she insists on her innocence?"

"She does indeed. She makes scenes all the time and insists there is a plot against her. I should say she was a very neurotic woman anyway, and this strain makes her worse. She will not face the facts and it is very difficult to get any assistance from her."

"I'll see to that." Sir Isambard's grin made him look even more like a bird of prey. "She'll talk to me all right."

He reflected for a moment. "I imagine that what the police consider their strong points are, firstly, the fact that Ada the housemaid saw her in the dining-room before dinner, and that she might have added ivy pollen to the salad then. But Ada didn't see her doing anything suspicious, and there was no reason why the woman shouldn't go into her own dining-room. Might be a perfectly innocent and harmless act. Damned fortunate no one saw her picking up the ivy pollen beforehand."

Mr. Henderson frowned at that, but said nothing.

"That's not very strong," continued Sir Isambard. "The second point is the cutting discovered by the snoopy tutor. That is uncomfortable. No jury is going to believe that it got there by accident. Somebody saw a note of the case in the London dailies and sent for the local paper because he or she thought there would be some useful information in a fuller account. And having got the useful information, used it.

"But the newsagent, from what you say, can't prove it was this woman herself who ordered it. We may be able to press him far enough to make him admit *any one* in the house might have ordered it. And that weakens the case considerably."

Sir Isambard meditated again.

"Anything against either Ada or snooper-tutor?" he asked.

"No. Nothing that I know of. Mrs. van Beer says they were both hateful and malicious and acted suspiciously, but so far as I can see she means nothing at all by that. She talks like that of everybody. They had no financial interest in the boy's death, either."

"Well, that leaves the Rodds and the child himself. For though the pointers the police have towards Mrs. van Beer aren't conclusive, they're pretty serious combined with the overwhelming motive. Unless we can show that other people could have done it and had reasons for doing it, we shall be in a tough spot.

"The Rodds get £4,000 as a result of the death. Mrs. Rodd could very easily have doctored the salad—more easily than any one else. Didn't you say there was some suspicion of Rodd stealing his employer's wine? It makes the pair look shady characters. Rodd might have ordered the Essex paper in his employer's name.

"A line there, I think.

"The child himself, too. From what you say of him, I'm inclined to think there's more hope there. The Rodds were well spoken of. You say yourself that you wouldn't believe they would have done the child any harm. But the boy was a very unhappy creature by your account, and you say he hated his aunt. I think it might be possible to persuade the jury that he intended to poison both himself and her, and died because of his weak constitution. We'll see what we can get out of the woman on those lines."

Sir Isambard became silent and soon afterwards fell asleep.

*

When they were introduced into the prison room where Mrs. van Beer was, Sir Isambard looked at her keenly. He saw a bedraggled woman of about fifty, with a lined and sagging face, and red eyes. She had dyed hair—golden—and a bad-tempered mouth. Her hands were quivering and she was obviously in a bad state of nerves.

As soon as the introduction was over, she went off like a firework.

"Well, I must say. It's time you came. I'm glad you've condescended to pay me some attention. You're costing me enough in money; I think I've paid for better service than this. You don't care how long I stay in gaol. You don't think for one minute of anything but your fees. I know you, Mr. Henderson; I've always known you. You think I'm a disgrace to the family and you'd have liked to do me out of my rights long ago. It's only because you couldn't that you're here now. The Arkwrights! That's all you care for."

Mr. Henderson was shocked, but he had obviously had this sort of thing before. "My dear lady," he said, "please be calm. Of course you are overstrained and we make every allowance for that. Believe me, we are doing all that we can do. Now, Sir Isambard Burns has very kindly come down all the way from London to go over the case with you. We need to ask you a few further questions."

"Very kindly come down all the way from London!" Mrs. van Beer sneered, and her voice became shrill. "Oh, thenks so very much," she minced. "I pay, don't I? You know everything already. I've answered and answered your questions till I'm sick. I'm not going to be messed about any more. You've got all the facts and you let me stay here, locked up on a trumped-up, nonsensical charge. You don't do anything. All you want to do is to hang things out as long as possible so as to increase your fees. You ought to be ashamed of yourselves."

Her voice was now a scream, and her sentences were punctuated with sobbing.

Mr. Henderson began a fresh soothing sentence, but Sir Isambard motioned him to silence.

"Mrs. van Beer," he said in the deep booming voice that had impressed so many courts. "I have certain questions to ask you. Will you or will you not answer them?"

"You get me out of here," she snuffled in answer. "That's your job. You know everything you need to know. Stop mucking me around. I'll show you *gentlemen*"—she snapped the word—"I won't be treated like this."

"Very well, then, Henderson," said Sir Isambard, "that settles that. There is no point in staying here. Mrs. van Beer, Mr. Henderson and I can have nothing more to do with your case. You must find some other advisers more to your liking. We shall not handle any case on such terms. I wish you goodmorning. Come along, Henderson."

Sir Isambard gathered up his hat and coat, and proceeded dignifiedly to the door. Mr. Henderson, after a momentary hesitation and in obvious distress, did the same.

Mrs. van Beer watched them in silence. As they neared the door she said in a less truculent tone:

"You won't leave me like this. I'm sorry if I spoke as I shouldn't have."

"Will you go first, Mr. Henderson?" said Sir Isambard with unusual punctiliousness, and ignoring Mrs. van Beer. Mr. Henderson walked through the door, unwillingly.

Rosalie van Beer put her hand out and half-rose. "Oh," she said in quite a different tone, "please don't go."

With that, her overtired nerves gave way and she began to cry in earnest. She laid her head on her hands on the table and wept quietly. Sir Isambard allowed her to cry: he realized the hysteria was working itself out. After a minute she lifted her head, and her ravaged face had acquired some dignity and a little calm.

"I'll do my best to answer," she said in a quiet tone. "I've no friends, and I've not had any for a long time. Sitting here alone, I get that frightened; and I've no one to turn to. It comes over me, and I don't know what I'm saying or doing. I'll be all right now; I will, I promise you."

Sir Isambard spoke more kindly, but still formally. He wished the interview to be as formal as might be; it would be less of a strain on her unreliable nerves. (How would she do in the witness box? He put that thought aside for later consideration.)

"This is a very trying time for you, Mrs. van Beer. No woman can go through what you are going through and not feel the strain. Believe me, we realize that. But we must all keep our heads. That is the only thing that will help us. Now, do you feel you can talk this over with me calmly now. Or shall Mr. Henderson get you a glass of water?"

"No. Thank you. I'm quite ready now."

"Excellent. Now first I should like to speak to you about the Rodds."

It was an unfortunate choice. Mrs. van Beer flushed and said, "They're thieves. Smooth-faced and—"

"Mrs. van Beer!" Sir Isambard's voice was gentle but he looked at her very firmly.

She bobbed her head forward at him deprecatingly. "I'm sorry. What did you want to know?"

"I have heard that Rodd is suspected of having stolen wine from your cellar. Do you know if that is the case? Did you suspect him of it?"

"I didn't suspect him of anything. I was always confiding with them. He told me all that wine was sour, and it was nasty stuff what I tasted, too. So I told him to throw it away and sell the bottles. I didn't know he'd been drinking it until the inspector caught him, and Mr. Henderson looked into it and found what he'd been up to." She looked at Mr. Henderson gratefully, trying to offer amends.

"You told him to throw it away and he drank it instead? H'm. How long had this been going on?"

"Years, I suppose. Since soon after Sir Henry died, anyway. Of course I don't know how fast and how often he drank it."

Sir Isambard drummed with two fingers on his own chin, a trick of his when puzzled. He decided to change the subject.

"Now I want to know about your relations with Philip. Did he dislike you?"

"I know that we ought never to speak evil of the dead; but he was a most *difficult* child. He was always—"

Sir Isambard looked at her sharply again. She stopped suddenly, and said, "What especially did you want to know?"

"I want to know of any concrete instances—actual instances, not general talk, mind—showing that he was either queer in his behaviour, or particularly evilly disposed to you."

Mrs. van Beer looked perplexed, as well she might. It would have been hard to find, among Philip's misdemeanours, anything that looked very serious now. Annoying the child had been, but she realized Sir Isambard needed something more than childish petulance. He tried again:

"Can you think of instances that other people saw? Something that either the Rodds, or the tutor, or Ada, or the doctor, saw. Something that shows him to have been rather unbalanced. I am wondering, you see, whether the poor boy may not have been so obsessed by a dislike of you that he tried to poison both himself and you. If he had been nursing such a desire, others may have seen something that pointed to a lack of balance. Try and think."

Mrs. van Beer made an effort. At last something presented itself to her mind.

"Well, there was a thing that happened just before the accident. The servants saw it, though them lying like they do I don't know what they'd say."

"Never mind: tell me."

"He made an attack on me with a knife in the kitchen and cut open my face. It was because the doctor had ordered me to destroy an unhealthy and diseased rabbit he had; and of course I had to do what the doctor said."

Mrs. van Beer proceeded to give her own account of the death of Philip's pet. Sir Isambard smiled and seemed highly pleased. Here was evidence of murderous intention enough, and it seemed that there might be corroboration.

"Tell me anything more you can about this rabbit," he said.

"A big savage thing it was. And you were asking was he ever queer in his behaviour; now, this is just what you want. Funny me not thinking of it before. It shows what a trained mind will do, you seeing how important it is and me knowing it all along and not having sense enough to understand." Mrs. van Beer had now brightened up and was almost her old self. "He used to pray to that rabbit, like. He used to recite things to it, and I found him one day kneeling in front of it and chanting like you do in church. That was the time he gave it that funny name."

"Devotion to a rabbit is common among children," said Sir Isambard disappointedly. "What sort of funny name was it, by the way?"

"Oh, I don't know," said Rosalie, deflated. "Something like Shreddy Vassar."

"Like what?" said Sir Isambard.

"I'll get it in a moment. I noticed it because it was so very queer." Mrs. van Beer hesitated. "Sredni Vashtar. That was it."

Sir Isambard looked deep in thought, but said nothing. After a minute he rose.

"Thank you, dear lady," he said. "You've given us a great deal of most valuable aid. And we shall be back to see you soon." He extended his hand.

PART III

Trial and Verdict

THE COURT

The Judge: Mr. Justice Stringfellow (Sir Alan Herbert Lemesurier Stringfellow).

The Accused: Rosalie van Beer, widow.

Leading Counsel for the Crown: Harold John Proudie, Esq., K.C.

Leading Counsel for the Defence: Sir Isambard Alexander Burns, Bt., K.C.

Foreman of the Jury: A. G. Popesgrove, Esq.

Remaining Jurors: Miss V. M. Atkins, Mrs. Morris, Dr. P. Holmes, Messrs. J. A. Stannard, E. Bryan, E. D. George, F. A. H. Allen, D. Elliston Smith, I. W. Drake, G. Parham Groves, and H. Wilson.

Clerk of Assize: Mr. P. J. Noble.

M R. PROUDIE DID NOT, NATURALLY, GIVE TO THE JURY ALL the details of Rosalie's life which we have just read. Some he did not know, anyhow: others he thought were superfluous. Her early background he sketched in very faintly, and indeed mercifully. He said scarcely anything of her unfortunate marriage to Mr. van Beer, and left the jury with no worse impression than that she had been a determined climber. Miss Atkins, ex-general servant, and Mr. Popesgrove, once a Thessalian waif, who had both risen from low beginnings to comfort, were prejudiced rather for than against her by the information; Mr. Bryan, shop assistant and fanatic, was indeed confirmed in a suspicion that Rosalie was a worldly woman, but he was uncomfortably realizing that he was surrounded by worldliness and that no person in the whole case, or in the court at all, was better than another. He was alone, a solitary Christian, and the hosts of Midian prowled and prowled around; yet his duty was not to defend himself against them—that he knew well enough how to do—but the grotesque task of separating one wolf from another and saying which was more wolfish, more blackly and thoroughly evil. The heart of mankind was in any case abominably wicked, unless it was redeemed, and to distinguish between grades of darkness was an almost impossible task. His dull grey eyes grew more perplexed as Mr. Proudie droned on; surely there would soon be a sign? But no sign came. He tried, imitating Mr. Popesgrove, the foreman, who was scribbling industriously, to take notes, but he had nothing to write down. He found himself drawing faces, an idle and frivolous occupation, and cast down his pencil angrily.

Mr. Proudie made very little of the manner of the discovery of the cutting from the *East Essex Monitor*. He did not even mention the tutor's name. It would come out in the evidence; meanwhile he was content to ascribe the discovery to the police "on information received". The description of the find was the first event in his speech, nevertheless, which made the jury alert. Each juror looked grave; Mr. Popesgrove stopped making notes and stared at Mr. Proudie with a fixed gaze of appraisal. Dr. Holmes felt a distinct sensation of relief. Here now was something that he could deal with. Up till that moment the course of events had displeased him. As a university don he had expected to be selected foreman, or if not that, at least to dominate the jury. There appeared to be no person of mature age who had anything like his educational qualifications. Some of his colleagues were probably not even gentlemen. There were actually two women, and Dr. Holmes, from his experience of Somerville and St. Hugh's students, was satisfied that their intelligence would be insufficient for them to grasp the essentials of the case at all. They would naturally require instruction and guidance, and it would be unlikely that any one but he could provide them. For after all he, and quite probably he alone, was skilled in dispassionately weighing of evidence. He considered himself a man of trained judgment. He was a scholar and had edited several Latin texts. To establish the correct readings in a corrupted author he had to go through a process which, he considered, was in all its essentials, judicial. Whenever he sat down to his work, he would have various editions by earlier scholars, commenting on the difficulties and offering their own solutions. All he had to do was to sit back and reflect. He would consider what authority should be attributed to each manuscript: he could by long experience trace back certain MSS. to one given archetype. If a group of MSS. continually presented the same errors, then they were all clearly copied from a single original. Therefore, their combined evidence added up to no more than one. Editors' conjectures, on the other hand, had to be judged by their innate plausibility alone. Thus he felt he had been for years trained in estimating the value of witnesses; the case would be child's play to him and he would be able swiftly to make up his mind and direct the rest of the jury.

But as Mr. Proudie told his story, and as he watched this rather common, uninteresting woman in the dock, Dr. Holmes had begun to realize that he was as much at sea as any other juror. You can interrogate classical manuscripts, in the proper sense of the word. You can ask them the same question again and again, and spend months considering their answer. And they will never change; their answer will always be the same. You can have as long as the publisher will allow you to consider your verdict (which is a lifetime, in the case of classical texts nowadays). But he realized that he could not treat spoken evidence in that way. He could not have it repeated at his pleasure. He could not even require Mr. Proudie to recapitulate his points whenever he needed to be reminded of them. Moreover, he had a very different question from his usual problems to answer. It was not: "What would a rather dirty-minded poet probably have written in the reign of Domitian?" but "How do ordinary human beings behave in times of stress? What did that unpleasant-looking woman over there probably do to a boy I have never seen?" And Dr. Holmes wondered if he really did know at all how ordinary people behave. His confidence began to fail him.

Now at last he was to be presented with a document. A piece of paper, which he could interrogate. Almost a manuscript. And very certainly a raft in a troubled sea. Relieved, he looked with renewed indulgence at his neighbour, that deplorable little man with the indigestion, whose eyes apologized to every one who would condescend to look his way.

The jury listened with equanimity to the opening evidence, which was medical. Dr. Lammas and Dr. Herrington described the cause and manner of death. It appeared that it was not going to be disputed that the boy Philip died from ivy poisoning. Only Mr. Popesgrove troubled to make notes; and this he did merely from a sense of duty. Some juror might ask him a question later, in the juryroom, and it would be his duty not only to be absolutely fair but fully equipped with all the information. Sir Isambard Burns, for the defence, asked no questions at all, though the woman in the dock repeatedly looked at him in an imploring manner.

Then Dr. Parkes was called. He looked very tired, old and nervous. The little white-haired man on the jury, Mr. Stannard, the public-house keeper, looked sympathetically upon this other little white-haired man. He didn't half look frightened. Would have bolted like a horse if he could, thought Mr. Stannard. And when Sir Isambard uncoiled his length and stood up to cross-examine, Dr. Parkes actually trembled; Mr. Stannard frowned in sympathy. If Dr. Parkes had been on trial he would have voted right away to acquit him; it wasn't fair to torment an old fellow. Anyway, he disliked that lawyer; the first beginning of an opinion formed in his mind.

Sir Ikey took a long time straightening himself out, and inserting his monocle into his eye. Ultimately he was ready.

"You have been practising a long time in these parts, Dr. Parkes?"

"Forty-five years."

"And you have many patients?"

"I don't see—I mean, it depends on what you call 'many'."

"Shall I put it this way: is your practice increasing or diminishing?"

"I don't know. I couldn't say." Dr. Parkes was a little indignant. "I suppose it is about the same."

"Indeed. An unusual ignorance for a man whose livelihood depends on the number of his clients. However, there is no doubt in your mind but that you had attended Philip Arkwright ever since he arrived here?"

"Certainly I had."

"And had a thorough knowledge of his condition of health?"

"I have said so."

"Yet you allowed thirty-six hours to pass when he was suffering from poisoning without applying any effective remedies. How was it you did not realize that his condition was abnormal?"

"You have heard other doctors say that the condition is a rare one and difficult to recognize."

"Other doctors who had not been attending the boy, and who would not have noticed anything unusual in his appearance. I am asking how you, who knew him exceptionally well, failed to notice his behaviour was abnormal?"

Dr. Parkes shrugged his shoulders and did not answer.

"Very well, we will leave that. Turn your mind back to the first day on which Philip's disease developed. On going back to your surgery did you consider the case any further?"

"Certainly I did. I always go over my cases every evening when I return. There always may be something…"

"Quite. Now did you then consider the question of poisoning? Did it enter your mind at all then?"

Dr. Parkes looked as if he had seen a snake. Sir Ikey had in fact no especial end in asking that question; he was merely feeling his way. But suddenly Dr. Parkes had seen himself fumbling about among his books in his surgery and taking one down—one that dealt with poisons. He remembered looking at it. He saw the first headings under A. *Antimony—Aconitine—Arsenic.* Had he gone on reading? Had he been interrupted? Had he forgotten? *And which day was it he had done that anyway?*

"We are waiting, Dr. Parkes."

"I—I," he stuttered. "I'm not sure."

"Not sure! Not sure!" Sir Ikey registered horror. "Haven't you searched your memory? Don't you regard this as important?"

"Of course I have. But I can't be certain."

"The next day your patient died of poisoning. Didn't you go over the whole case in your mind at once, Dr. Parkes? Didn't it occur to you to wonder where you had made your mistake? Didn't you even then ask yourself when you first suspected poisoning?"

"Yes. I must have done."

"I see. You must have done. But now you have forgotten. I hope you are not often so forgetful. It is a bad thing for a doctor to be." Sir Ikey sneered: he had a good sneer. "Still you did think of poisoning some time; that is something. Let us consider the next day. You saw Philip in the morning. I think you said about 9.15?"

"Yes."

"You are sure of that?"

"Of course I am."

"Ah, yes. That was written in your book. And you came back with Dr. Herrington at 12.15?"

"I believe so."

"Three hours! Three hours, with the child vomiting blood, and his heart obviously weakening. What on earth were you doing? Why were you not by his bedside?"

"I had great difficulty in making contact with Dr. Herrington. He was out on his rounds."

"Well? Could you not leave telephone messages for him, to bring him to you urgently? How could you leave the unhappy boy to two utterly unskilled women? What did you do in fact?"

Dr. Parkes remained dumb. What had he done? He was already a little confused in his memory. He thought he had driven round looking for Herrington. All he was certain of was that he had decided the case was beyond his powers: that he could be of no use till a younger man came. And that he would not say.

Sir Ikey glared at him.

"In plain language, Doctor, if you had dealt with this case properly the child would be alive to-day. Is not that so?"

"It is wholly untrue."

"Oh. And why, pray?"

"The condition was incurable."

"Incurable! How are you able to say such a thing? I thought you had told the court you knew very little about the effects of hederin."

"I mean—I—"

"You mean, I think, that *you* do not know of any remedy. How long ago did you qualify, Dr. Parkes?"

"Really!" Dr. Parkes flushed.

"I think, Sir Isambard—" said the judge; and did not finish his remark. Sir Ikey bowed: he bowed very straight and stiff, from far down and as if he had a hinge in his hips. "As your lordship pleases," he said. "I have no further questions," he added.

Mr. Proudie re-examined, and again brought out the point that hederin poisoning was rare and difficult to recognize. But Sir Ikey had made his point. "Doctor a fool," wrote Dr. Holmes on his writing-pad, and expressed the opinion of most of his fellow-jurors. Even Mr. Stannard sighed and shook his head.

2

THE NEXT WITNESS WHO LEFT HER MARK ON THE JURY WAS Mrs. Rodd. Dressed in deep black, with her squat figure and homely face, she favourably impressed the jurors even before her evidence began. Here, they all felt, was a sound, respectable cook; an honest, kindly woman on whom they could rely. Even her wart with its tuft of hair seemed to add to her reliability. She spoke in a firm but respectful voice, the voice of a servant who knew her place, and whose place was one worth having. Mr. Proudie, not always aware of histrionic possibilities, nevertheless built up her character as the loyal old retainer as thoroughly as Sir Ikey himself could have done.

"I think you were cook to the late Sir Henry Arkwright?" he said in a rather hushed voice, as if reluctant to recall to Mrs. Rodd what must have been one of the great deprivations of her life.

"Yes, sir; I was." Mrs. Rodd spoke gently and nodded—no, better, bowed her head.

"And for how many years did you occupy this post?"

It was a good beginning, and Mrs. Rodd was intelligent enough to play up. When she went on to describe Philip's relations with his aunt, and the affair of the rabbit, Mr. Proudie had but little to do. The story itself moved the jury enough. Dr. Holmes alone resisted it as sentimental. Mrs. Morris, the Jewish widow, to her extreme astonishment found her eyes swimming. She had never cried since Les died. She *could not* cry, that she knew. And yet there were tears in her eyes and one trickling down the side of her nose and itching. The poor, poor little boy, sitting on his heels and crooning to his rabbit because he had no other friend. And those stupid clothes! Mrs. Rodd had described the Norfolk suit, not without some malice; but Mrs. Morris was the only juror on whom the description had its effect. To make the poor child deliberately a guy! Mrs. Morris cast an angry look at Rosalie, but she held her face down and her expression could not be seen.

Mrs. Rodd was describing in detail the killing of the rabbit in the gas oven. It lost nothing in brutality when she told it. As she described Philip's hysteria over its death, Mrs. Morris again felt discomfort. Poor lonely child, she thought. I've never had a child. I could have looked after him. I'd have understood. That woman took away from him the only thing he loved and killed it. I know what that means. It's not absurd, it's a real comparison. A child can love very desperately: it can feel very deeply for a time. It just doesn't last so long, that's all. That boy might quite well have loved his rabbit, allowing for difference in age and all that, like I loved ——. Stop that. Listen to what the defence lawyer is saying.

Sir Ikey, oddly enough, did not seem to be trying to undo Mr. Proudie's work. If anything, he was underlining Philip's affection for the rabbit. But he brought out one point which was the only one to date that seemed to help his client. What caused Mrs. van Beer to kill the rabbit? Mrs. Rodd rather reluctantly admitted that she understood it to be the doctor's orders. No, she hadn't heard him say so herself.

"Perhaps we can have Dr. Parkes recalled to prove that point?" Sir Ikey addressed his inquiry half to the judge and half to Mr. Proudie.

The judge looked at Mr. Proudie. "Certainly," said the latter. "We will be very glad to oblige my learned friend."

"I have a couple more questions to ask this witness," said Sir Ikey. "Perhaps I may finish with her first?"

The judge nodded.

"Do you remember the name of this rabbit, Mrs. Rodd?"

"Yes, sir. He used to call it King Zog, but he'd just changed its name to something else. A funny name."

"Try and think. Can you remember it?"

"It was something like Shredny Vashti—Vashti like the queen in the Bible, you know; that's how I remembered it."

"Something like Shredny Vashti. Now I don't want to put the words in your mouth, Mrs. Rodd, but tell me this: was it Sredni Vashtar?"

"Yes, sir. That was it. That was exactly what it was."

"Thank you. That is all."

Dr. Parkes, recalled, faced Sir Ikey with visible uneasiness. But this time the vulture did not swoop. Sir Ikey spoke gently.

"You remember this affair of the rabbit, Dr. Parkes?"

"Yes. Yes."

"Did you in fact order the destruction of the animal?"

"Well, no. No, I do not think I could say that exactly. Perhaps I should explain in greater detail. If I might."

"Please do."

"The boy's health was far from good, and I was worried because he never managed to pick up his strength as he should. I considered a number of possible influencing causes. In particular, his aunt directed my attention to his habit of keeping animals in a rather dirty condition, and fondling them. I thought this rather insanitary—"

"I am sorry to interrupt you, but I would like to ask you here: was his aunt's solicitousness for his health usual? Or was this an exceptional intervention of hers?"

"Not at all exceptional. She was very concerned about Philip's health. She always was. Not a doubt on that question. She paid the greatest possible attention to it."

"Thank you." Sir Ikey's thanks appeared quite genuine. He turned to the jury, dropped his monocle and with his eyebrows invited them to notice the doctor's words. "Pray proceed. I apologize for interrupting."

"I warned Philip that if he continued to nurse this animal and to run the risk of infection from it, it might have to be taken from him. My intention was not to order its destruction. I saw no definite evidences of disease, and I did not intend anything so drastic. Looking back, however, I see that perhaps my words might have been misinterpreted. I think it quite possible that Mrs. van Beer might have understood me to... to have given a more explicit order than I had meant to do."

"I understand. One other question. Do you happen to know the rabbit's name?"

"Its *name*?"

"Yes. There is an object in this question, I assure you."

"I am pretty certain that Philip gave it the name which you mentioned in this court a little while ago."

"Sredni Vashtar?"

"Yes."

Sir Ikey screwed his monocle into his eye and offered the witness to Mr. Proudie. Mr. Proudie shook his head, deciding to let ill alone. Dr. Parkes stood down, and Sir Ikey smiled with the expression of a pin-table enthusiast who has won a packet of cigarettes.

Mrs. Morris, on the jury, looked contemptuous. That woman solicitous for the child's health indeed. Any one could see the doctor was a fool. It would need someone cleverer than him to cover that woman's wickedness up. She killed an innocent animal to torture a little boy. She may have pretended she was doing it for his own good. That only made it worse. Hypocrite.

Dr. Holmes, on the other hand, thought it showed good sense. Children he didn't like, and pet animals he liked less. To get rid of a pet animal that probably smelt seemed to him a thoroughly sensible action. So far as he was concerned the story of the rabbit was by now wholly to the accused's credit.

None of the other jurors showed by their faces what their opinions on it were, if any.

Despite the descriptions in detective novels, court cases are rarely dramatic. For one five-minute scene there are hours of dull and formal proceedings. Even in murder trials this is true and *R. v. van Beer* was no exception. The jury grew tired as the day went on. It received the news that the court was rising for lunch with obvious gratitude. They were taken to lunch under the escort of a bailiff and at the expense of the under sheriffs of the city. Mr. George, the trade union official, protested vehemently. The men at Trollope and Colls might well have walked out that morning; and the chairman in that case would certainly have gone round and pledged the union's full support. He had absolutely reckoned on going to his office in the lunch-hour and putting things straight. Ultimately he had to content himself with a long telephone call, from which he returned with a long face. Mr. Stannard thought unhappily that Gwen and Fred would find the lunch-hour rush too much for them, but he was not allowed to go back to his pub.

Conversation at lunch was limited and formal, for Mr. Popesgrove killed the most promising subject as soon as it was broached. Mr. Allen, the young Socialist, asked his neighbour in a loud voice what he thought of the case. Mr. Popesgrove intervened very civilly but firmly. "I say," he said. "You know, I don't want to interfere, but do you think that's quite wise? Wouldn't it be better if we didn't discuss it at all until we'd heard the other side? It's so likely that in conversation we shall begin to take sides, and there we are making up our minds on only part of the evidence. Honestly, I do think we'd better talk about something else."

Mr. Allen was surprised and abashed. "Sorry," he said.

3

THE FIRST WITNESS THEY HEARD ON THEIR RETURN WAS the newsagent near the Red Lion in Wrackhampton. By now he had veered to the opinion that Rosalie van Beer had ordered the *East Essex Monitor* in person. No, he was not sure. He thought it likely but couldn't be positive. Yes, it was true that his wife had held a different idea, but when they looked up their other bills about the same date it had refreshed their memory.

"Wretched witness," muttered Dr. Holmes. "Can't make up his mind and goes on chattering."

Sir Ikey let him go fairly quickly. Nor did he spend much time on Sergeant Knowles's account of the discovery of the cutting. He cross-examined Ted Gillingham when he appeared about his own share in it, but largely out of malice, with questions such as these:

"Tell me what is your usual procedure in going into someone else's rooms, Mr. Gillingham?"

"Do you habitually go through the books to see if there are any documents in them?"

"Is there anything else you do—do you open drawers? Take letters out of their envelopes, for example?"

Gillingham protested, and was in the end protected by the judge. Sir Ikey again bowed from the hinge in his back, and accepted the rebuke quite placidly.

"Well, we will take it then, Mr. Gillingham, that you did not snoop around—I think that is the usual word—snoop around to any great extent. You went almost at once to this book, and there you found that cutting?"

"Yes."

"Had you often been in that room before?"

"Fairly often, I should say."

"You knew your way about all right?"

"Why, yes."

"Had you been there alone before?"

"I suppose so."

"You had been there alone before. And you went straight to that particular book in a not inconsiderable library; and you found this peculiar cutting. Very curious! Mr. Gillingham"—Sir Isambard's voice became very clear and loud—"*had you ever seen that cutting before?*"

"No, certainly not! What do you mean?" replied Gillingham, scarlet with embarrassment and surprise, and looking thoroughly guilty.

"Never mind what I mean," said Sir Ikey, who indeed did not mean anything in particular, but hoped only to start some irrelevant doubt in the mind of a stupid juror. "You are here to answer questions, not to ask them."

Mr. Proudie re-examined, and drew out the fact that by no means could the tutor have any interest in the conviction of Mrs. van Beer or in the death of Philip Arkwright. But the harm was not wholly undone. The jury as a whole had an irritating doubt whether everything was quite normal about Gillingham's discovery of the newspaper cutting. Even Dr. Holmes reminded himself that in judging a document one must consider not only its text but its provenance. Mr. Stannard began to say aloud that there was something fishy about that business, when he remembered that jurors did not chatter during a case. Miss Atkins reflected that those that hide can find. In no one's mind was there any defined opinion, but at the back of every one's thoughts there was implanted a slight uneasiness. In other words, Sir Ikey had done what he wished to do.

Sir Henry's will was put in evidence. There was no dispute about its terms, or its meaning. It was a signpost pointing towards Rosalie, who inherited a fortune. But it pointed also towards the Rodds, who got £4,000 altogether. A fortune for them, too. Mr. Popesgrove, forgetting his own precepts about making up one's mind on only part of the evidence, wrote on his note-pad: *"Accident appears ruled out. Therefore murder. Will indicates only three possible murderers: two servants, Mrs. V. B. Mrs. V. B. has greater motive. Essential evidence now required—opportunity, means. Newspaper cutting only proves premeditation of some person, not of who."* He crossed out "who" and replaced it by "whom".

Ada Corney's evidence, which followed, provided him with the evidence he was asking for. Mrs. van Beer had been in the dining-room in the interval between the laying of the table and the commencement of lunch. The salad had been washed thoroughly beforehand by the cook, and when it came out after dinner she, Ada, noticed that it was gritty. She gave her evidence in a slow and sullen way, her mouth with its bad teeth hanging slightly open between sentences. She looked unhealthy—her face was pasty, and an inflamed spot on the side of her chin had burst and was discharging—and she looked stupid, but she knew what she had to say and Sir Ikey could not shift her from it.

She was the last witness for the prosecution, and she seemed to be final in more senses than one. Means, motive, opportunity, premeditation—all four seemed to be proved. Mr. Popesgrove added the whole thing up in his mind. A hard-hearted and cruel woman, who disliked the sickly boy. A fortune for her if he died. The means to hand, scattered all over the garden path. And not only was it proved that she secured the information on how to use it, but she was seen in the room when the doctoring of the food must have been done. Short of an actual eyewitness of her poisoning the child, there could be no stronger evidence.

He looked at his notes and checked them over, almost in the same way as he was accustomed to check over all the restaurant accounts. The result seemed to come to the same every time.

4

Y ET SIR IKEY, AS HE ROSE, SEEMED QUIETLY CONFIDENT.
Quietly indeed was hardly the word; he was if anything flam-
boyant. He spread his hands on the table in front of him, leaning
on them, until they splayed out like claws, he fixed his eyeglass
to one side of his long nose and let his glance travel slowly along
the jury, pass by the judge and settle on the pink plump upturned
face of Mr. Proudie. He looked rather like an eagle which had
perceived an unusually fat and helpless rabbit, and, sure of its prey,
was pleasurably hesitating before it swooped.

"As I listened," he said at last, "to my learned friend, I admired
his skill more than I had ever done before. As he spoke, and as he
marshalled his evidence, I myself believed for a moment that he
had a case. You may not know, ladies and gentlemen of the jury,
but we who follow this little-loved profession of the law have to
know, that my learned friend is reputed one of the most dangerous persons at the Bar. His skill at presenting his case is almost
legendary: he can make his bricks not merely without straw, but
without clay and without water. To-day, indeed, he has nothing
but straws, and these are few, damaged, and pointing in the wrong
direction."

Dr. Holmes sniggered, and the jury began to thaw.

"I shall call but little evidence, and I propose to explain to you
why. Briefly, my reason is that most of the evidence that you have
heard answers itself. This you will see on reflection. Perhaps, at
any rate before you have heard what I have to say, you may have

a residue of suspicion in your mind. But his lordship will tell you that that is not enough. Suspicion is bound to be spread around after so shocking an incident as the death of this unfortunate boy. So widespread was it, and so reckless were the tongues that wagged, that it was found necessary to change the venue of this trial to London, as I expect most of you know, for the especial purpose of securing an impartial trial.

"Nor is it necessary, as his lordship will confirm to you, for the defence to prove that someone else committed a murder, and to name who that someone else was. It is for the prosecution to prove firstly that there was a murder, and secondly that my client committed it. Both of these things, as is becoming clear to you, I hope, it has failed to do. And even had it put up a plausible case on both these points, the whole structure would collapse were we able to prove that other persons could very well have done the murder—had both opportunity and motive. This we can do.

"Let me deal briefly with the most obvious point. Was there a murder at all? I am far from satisfied on this point, and so I expect are you. You all, I think, perceived the demeanour of Dr. Parkes in the box, and I hope you noticed the conclusion to be drawn from his admission. For well over twenty-four hours he failed to realize the condition of his patient and applied remedies which were wholly unsuited to the case. He did not call in another doctor until the unfortunate child was literally *in extremis* and all help was vain. For all practical purposes—I am aware this is a harsh statement, but it is my duty to speak plainly—for all practical purposes the boy was unattended until the moment of death. Had a more competent doctor been in charge of the case, who can say what the result would have been? I believe that most of you feel, as I do, that but for this accident Philip Arkwright might well be alive to-day."

Sir Ikey spoke clearly and simply, not raising his voice or using the deep booming tones that sometimes confounded over-confident witnesses. He next turned to Mrs. Rodd. He showed that she had an excellent motive. Four thousand pounds to herself and her husband—vast wealth to persons in their position. The salad was made by her, and thrown away by her. She did not need to go into the dining-room to doctor the dressing—it was the product of her hands and she could have done what she chose with it at almost any time. No doubt she had washed the salad, as the maid Ada said. What of it? She would not serve the lettuce dirty, in any case. Had she been going to mix ivy dust in the dressing, that would certainly have been done when the salad was washed and ready.

"Then there is the incident of the discovery of this cutting, which is supposed to bear hardly upon my client. Ladies and gentlemen, what a peculiar story this is! Have you ever heard an odder one? Let us ask first of all where it came from. The answer is: No one knows. You heard the newsagent. First of all he or his wife thought it was Mrs. Rodd's husband. But now—after weeks have passed in which the whole neighbourhood has been one mass of seething, unreflecting prejudice against my client—he has decided that it was ordered by her. However, even now he will not swear. He just thinks it might be so. A worthless statement—a mere opinion—nothing whatever. In cold fact, we don't know who acquired this paper. It might be any one—Mr. Rodd, Mrs. Rodd, even Mr. Gillingham, the inquisitive teacher.

"And how was it discovered? I wish I had been there. I listened to Mr. Gillingham, as you did, and I marvelled. Here is a considerable library, books of all kinds and many of them. He denies that he snooped around. No, he goes straight to the shelves, and out of all those hundreds of books picks down one, a little-used one, which happens to contain this peculiarly convenient document. How did he come to see it? He doesn't know. Was it thrust forward on the shelf a little, so as to attract his attention? Was an edge of the document enticingly poking out? Had it been arranged there—planted, I believe is the word—so as to be certain to be found by the first comer? 'Don't know, don't know, don't know'—that is all he can say; and all we can say.

"What we know amounts to precisely this. Some person, whose identity is quite unknown, purchased a copy of the *East Essex Monitor,* part of which was found, for reasons which are not explained, in a book where it had been for a time whose length is quite uncertain. What does that mean, gentlemen? It means this and no more: that any one—any one at all—who visited that house may have known that a sufficient dose of ivy dust was a dangerous thing. It is not proved that every one in the house did know this. It is not proved that other persons did not know this already. For example, Rodd the gardener, who presumably knows all the local lore of herbs and plants. Or his wife, who prepared the salad. Either of these may have known anyway.

"What do we know about this? I asked. The answer seems to be: we know nothing at all.

"I might well leave the question at that, and ask you to acquit my client without further ado. But though it is no part of my duty to find the guilty person for the prosecution, the probable solution of the mystery seems to me so evident that I feel it my duty to touch upon it. It may be that no crime was committed. I cannot, despite the evidence of the police-sergeant, feel certain in my own mind that the ivy dust which is presumed to have been in the salad did not come there accidentally. But let us suppose that there has been a crime. Then, in that case, there is but little doubt that the responsible person is now beyond our reach.

"Let us look over the conditions in this house at the time of the tragedy, and see if we can find where there was any sufficient anger or hatred to lead to so awful an act. We have the two Rodds, whose behaviour may have been equivocal, but whom we will lay aside for the moment. We have the aunt, whose whole record is one of continual anxiety over her nephew's health. Dr. Parkes remembered very little, but of one thing he was quite sure. He was certain that she was continually calling him in and watching over the boy's condition. The prosecution, I may point out to you, have given no explanation of why this lady, who admittedly had for years worried—more than worried, *fussed* over Philip Arkwright's health, should suddenly have destroyed the life she had so anxiously preserved. And then we have the boy himself— sickly, abnormal, and given to sudden rages. He has gone where we cannot question him, and only Dr. Parkes, whose qualifications you will have estimated for yourselves, attended him and can report in detail. But I shall lay before you some expert interpretation of his state of mind; so far as that can be deduced from the medical evidence of the witnesses for the prosecution. I shall not produce any other evidence: I propose, for scrupulous fairness, to use only the evidence of my opponents."

Sir Ikey did not mention that this was no real concession, as the medical witnesses for the prosecution were not only the only possible witnesses, but had given evidence that was very suitable for his purpose.

"In this small household a minor tragedy occurs. The boy's pet is destroyed. I hope no one of you is going to judge Mrs. van Beer harshly for this. Say that she was over-officious, if you like. If every parent or guardian who is over-officious is to be considered a criminal, then our courts will work overtime. At least, Dr. Parkes has admitted that she may well have considered his words to constitute a more precise instruction than he meant at the time. She may have been inconsiderate, but one thing admits of no doubt—she believed that in taking this action she was safeguarding the child's health. She may have been harsh; I do not think she was. She may have been unwise; in view of the terrible but unforeseeable results I believe that she herself would admit she was. But what is quite certain is this, that she was moved by nothing but a meticulous and anxious thought for her charge's welfare.

"Well, right or wrong, she has the pet destroyed. The highly strung, unhappy child is shocked by the death of the animal to whom he was devoted. You have heard Dr. Parkes, Mrs. Rodd, and the tutor all confirm the unhealthy, passionate adoration which he had for it. And what happens then? He finds, as anybody else might have done, a cutting in the reading-room which shows him a way to revenge. He will punish this too-strict aunt who has taken away his darling. His small mind temporarily unbalanced with anger, he gathers some ivy dust and scatters it secretly over the food, probably over the salad. He eats very little himself but sees with glee his aunt, the destined victim, make her usual healthy meal. So he will suffer some little inconveniences and she will die.

"But alas for the plans of eleven-year old plotters! Philip had not allowed for the reaction of the human body. His aunt's frame rejected the poison—she had eaten but too heartily from his point of view, and her healthy stomach threw back the deadly dose. He had eaten much less and his frame was in a morbid condition and less able to tell good from evil. The poison stayed in his body. A child's memory is very uncertain and very irregular. It is quite likely, as those of you who have families will agree, that by the afternoon he had wholly forgotten his carefully planned revenge on his aunt. When he first felt the pangs of the poison he may have considered them only to be an attack of his recurrent stomach trouble. If he did remember, he was unable to tell any one, for, young though he was, he must have realized he had done a very wrong thing. He may have thought that the doctor in any case would know what to do. I think we may presume that he had a child's all-embracing and implicit faith in his family practitioner. Nor was he unjustified, for had he been treated properly I am convinced he might well have survived.

"All this, you will say, is plausible—it is even probable. But it is reconstruction, it is not ascertained fact. Have you any direct evidence? Ladies and gentlemen, we have. Philip Arkwright himself left behind direct evidence of his desires and intentions, as clear and definite as a written confession for those who can read it.

"That evidence, you may be surprised to hear, depends upon the name of the rabbit. You may have wondered why I was so insistent on establishing the exact form of that curious name, out of the unwilling mouths of hostile witnesses. You are about to hear the reason. And to explain this I am putting in as evidence this book."

He showed the jury a small blue book whose title they could not read.

"It is not an unused book which mysteriously leapt out to the hand of an inquisitive visitor. It is a much-used book from the late Sir Henry's library, which occupied a prominent place on a low shelf. It was found by the solicitor for the defence, a highly respected gentleman by the name of Archibald Henderson, in the presence of the witnesses, whom you will hear. And he found it because he was looking for it.

"However, this is enough of my remarks. You need to hear the evidence, and I will call it."

5

S IR IKEY, CORRECTLY JUDGING THAT NONE OF THE JURORS
would have read "Saki", chose to adjourn the explanation of
the rabbit's name while he presented the evidence of Dr. Richard
Taylor, of Harley Street, who had made a fortune as a "straight"
doctor and taken up psychiatry afterwards. He combined the
enthusiasm of a devotee (for he earnestly believed Dr. Freud to
be the greatest man of the century) with the smooth authorita-
tive manner which had brought him to the top of his original
profession. His book *Masochism and International Politics* had had
a success sufficient to convince him that he could handle any
ideological or political group. Young Mr. Allen, the poet-Socialist
on the jury, had read it and believed it. Whatever Dr. Taylor said
was assured beforehand of his assent if it was in any way possible.

Sir Ikey purred at the doctor. He ascertained that he had heard
all the evidence given at that trial concerning Philip's state of
mind. He had also read all the evidence at the inquest. He had
had the pleasure of prolonged conversations with Dr. Parkes.
Had he formed an opinion concerning the mental state of the
deceased child? He had. Was that opinion consistent with the
possibility of the boy having conceived a plan to poison his aunt
in the manner suggested? It was. Perhaps Dr. Taylor would be
willing to explain to the jury more in detail the child's probable
condition of mind? He would.

Dr. Taylor had undistinguished features, but very shiny black
hair, smoothed and greased back from his forehead. His manner

was that of one explaining simply to men who were his intellectual
equals a matter of which they happened merely not to know the
facts, but which they would at once understand when he had given
them the original, relatively unimportant historical data. He used
repeatedly words that they half-understood, like "complex", or
which they did not understand at all, like "trauma"; but he used
them invariably in sentences of the simplest construction which
were apart from them composed wholly of common Anglo-Saxon
derivatives. They felt in each case that they had nearly understood
what he said, and that if they had only paid more attention to the
context they would have understood it altogether.

He described the causation and symptoms of fetichism and
their possible bearing on this case. He concluded that on the
whole they had no direct bearing, but that certain analogies and
certain behaviour-patterns might be held in mind, as illustrations
and not as proof. He mentioned the Oedipus complex, with an
apologetic lift of the eyebrows, as of one who has to introduce
hackneyed and misused quotations into a sophisticated audience;
he reminded them that owing to the death of the parents a transference of emotions to the aunt might be legitimately presumed.
He found no immediately visible evidences of schizophrenia,
but he would not dismiss it wholly. The relations of the boy to
the rabbit, on the other hand, gave incontrovertible proof of
his masochism.

The last statement seemed to be connected with Philip's
semi-deification of his pet, but the jury as a whole was by now
too confused to analyse its impression. The boy was loopy, as
Miss Victoria Atkins noted, and that was the main thing. Not
so Mr. Proudie: he thought that he had discovered a flaw in the

defence's case which he could prise open into a wide split. He took his chance as soon as the time came for cross-examination.

"You said, Dr. Taylor, that you deduced evidences of maso-chism in Philip Arkwright?"

"I did."

"You indicated, did you not, that this was really the guiding indication to his behaviour? I am sorry if I do not use the correct technical terms: I hope I make myself clear, at least."

"Yes, I think that that is more or less the meaning of what I said."

"Masochism, as I understand it, is an unhealthy desire to submit to suffering?"

"Unhealthy is a question-begging term. Are you able to define mental health? I am not, and I fancy I have had considerable experi-ence. But if you will substitute the word 'pathological' I will not object to your statement."

"Very well: pathological. That does not affect my point. The child, you say, wished to be dominated, wished to be oppressed, even to the extent of worshipping a rabbit." (Mr. Proudie's tones expressed the contempt of the plain man for such high-faluting chatter; his eyebrows invited the jury to join him in the ranks of men of simple good sense.) "Possibly, possibly. But I am won-dering how you reconcile the later events with your hypothesis. Sir Isambard has suggested—I say suggested, for no trace of evidence has yet appeared—that the boy plotted to poison his aunt and by some mistake poisoned himself. This is not the act of a masochist—not the act of one who desires to be the victim of suffering. It is the act of the very opposite. In the words of your own profession—we are not wholly illiterate in this court,

Dr. Taylor," (Mr. Proudie's archness caused a slight flush to appear on the doctor's face) "—in the words of the average psychological essay, it is the act of a sadist. The precise opposite of a masochist, is it not, Doctor?"

"That particular state of mind," replied Dr. Taylor, openly cross, "is what you would call ambivalent." (Mr. Proudie's pink podgy hands waved away any acquaintance with such a word.) "Masochistic phenomena transpose themselves into sadistic with a minimum of difficulty. So far from such a transference being a difficulty to my explanation, it is of the essence of it. I am sorry if I did not make myself clear."

"You did not. May I ask you to put in one sentence—clearly if you can—what you think Philip's state of mind was?"

"Certainly. He was a concealed sado-masochist," said Dr. Taylor, with the air of one firing off a Big Bertha.

After him came Mr. Henderson, dry and not worried by any cross-examination from Mr. Proudie. He identified the blue book. It was a volume of short stories by H. H. Munro, who wrote under the name of "Saki". He had found it in the house, on a low shelf well within the reach of a boy of eleven. It had obviously been read. It contained a story entitled *Sredni Vashtar*.

Sir Ikey then took the book in his hands. He did not intend to leave the reading of this story to the clerk of the court. He was going to use his organ voice for the first time in this case. Mr. Ramsay MacDonald had become prime minister for little more than possessing a voice hardly any better than his. Could he not by the same means secure the acquittal of one unimportant woman? "This book," he said to the jury "will be placed in your hands, but before that I wish, with the permission of the court, to read aloud to you the brief story from which Philip Arkwright took the name of his pet."

He cleared his throat and began:

"SREDNI VASHTAR.

"'Conradin was ten years old, and the doctor had pronounced his professional opinion that the boy would not live another five years...'"

H. H. Munro's story is one of the most cruel written by that politely cruel author. It is about a sickly boy who had an aunt whom he detested, and who interfered with him continually for his own good. As Sir Ikey read it, it seemed an exact reproduction, in the eyes of an embittered child, of Philip's relation to Mrs. van Beer. The analogy was sharpened by the fact that Mrs. De Ropp, the aunt in the story, had a name whose sound recalled that of Mrs. van Beer's: Sir Ikey's voice hesitated over it and drew out the similarity. Munro's story was admirably suited to his object. It was itself written in recollection of a childish hatred not unlike Philip's: the author in his youth had been under the charge of an aunt named Augusta, who had bullied and oppressed him, and years afterwards he had revenged himself in drawing her portrait and assigning to her the fate that he may often have prayed for her.

Conradin in his story had two pets—one a Houdan hen, whatever that may be, one a large polecat-ferret. "One day," Saki wrote, "out of heaven knows what material, he spun the beast a wonderful name, and, from that moment, it grew into a god and a religion." The name he invented for it was Sredni Vashtar.

His aunt had the Houdan hen destroyed, and from that time on Conradin prayed a prayer to Sredni Vashtar. He did not say in his prayer what he wanted, for a god knows all and need not be told. But one day his aunt suspected he was keeping things in the greenhouse, and said she would have them cleared away, whatever they were. Conradin watched her from the window, hoping for a miracle but believing that shortly she would have the ferret brought out by the gardener and taken away. But time went on: she did not come out. And in the end "out through that doorway came a long, low, yellow-and-brown beast, with eyes a-blink at the waning daylight, and dark wet stains around the fur of jaws and throat".

The story ended with Conradin comfortably making himself a piece of buttered toast while the maids twitter outside the nursery door, wondering who will get up courage enough to tell him that his beloved aunt is dead.

"Sredni Vashtar," said Sir Ikey, fixing with his eye Dr. Holmes who looked, and for the minute was, completely convinced by this reading. "Sredni Vashtar. That is not a name that can be invented twice by accident. When we find that the book in which this strange name occurs was within reach of the child's hand, we do not need to ask for any further explanation. We have put clearly before us precisely what he thought of his aunt, precisely what fate he intended for her. He thought of his rabbit as a sort of god. She killed it; she was to suffer the fate that the woman in the story suffered. There is no other explanation of this peculiar name. No other explanation at all: I can safely defy the prosecution to produce one."

6

M R. STANNARD, ON THE JURY, HAD HOPED THAT ROSALIE would give evidence, and that he could make up his mind by watching her, but he was to be disappointed. Not until the last moment had Sir Ikey made up his mind to keep her out of the witness box, but on the day itself he had been definite. He had gone to great pains to groom her for the ordeal. He had given her precise orders on the clothes that she was to wear, even the amount of lipstick she was to put on, and had gone over her evidence with her again and again. He was well aware, too, of the prejudice a jury has against a defendant who doesn't give evidence. However explicitly the judge tells them that in a murder case it is the defendant's absolute right and that they are to draw no deductions from it, however carefully prosecuting counsel refrains from mentioning it, still the jurors say, "Ah, the prisoner had something to conceal. Else why not stand up honestly and tell the truth?" But he had reluctantly decided it was not safe. Let her loose, and she would do all she could to hang herself. Even in the prison room with him she seemed to him unstable: out in court and harried by a clever counsel she would lose her control entirely. He could see her shrilling her spite against the Rodds, and alternately spraying false sentiment over the dead child and letting it be seen how much she disliked him in fact. He had told Mr. Henderson brutally that she had "too little sense and was incapable of being honest". Mr. Henderson had translated that to his client in the words: "Sir Isambard has decided the strain would be too great for you."

Nevertheless, Sir Ikey thought it wiser to make an effort to present a pleasing picture of his client to the jury. Some evidence other than the prosecution's had better be obtained. Proudie's witnesses alone would leave too disagreeable an impression. It had not been very easy: Rosalie had not been liked in the neighbourhood, and anyway both enemies and friends had to admit that they knew very little of her way of life. Ultimately, only the vicar could be found. Originally, when Rosalie had come to the district, he had been reasonably assiduous: his wife had called on her, and she had been invited to tea at the vicarage. But gradually, because her vulgarity and her whining irritated him, he had begun to drop her; he was uncomfortably aware that the fact that she did not subscribe largely to church funds had something to do with this. For this he blamed himself; and he blamed himself even more that the tragedy had occurred at all. Wherever the chief guilt lay, some guilt at least lay with him; for there had obviously been great spiritual illness in that house, and he, the spiritual healer and adviser by right and duty, had known nothing of it. Illogically, therefore, but naturally, he atoned for his neglect and unworthy thoughts about Mrs. van Beer by overpraising her now. The testimonial he gave to her as a Christian woman and devoted guardian was based on very little real evidence.

Mr. Proudie was sufficiently well informed not to let it pass. He examined the vicar fairly closely about his relations with Mrs. van Beer, and showed that she had had less and less contact with him of recent months, and that she had even given up attending church regularly. He had undone most of the effect of the vicar's compunction, when there was a sudden interruption.

Edward Bryan, the fanatic on the jury, had been waiting and silently praying for guidance. Hour after hour had passed, only adding to his darkness, and at last he had realized that illumination would not come to him by dispensation and without any action of his own. It was Providence's intention that he should find the sign for himself; he must strain his mind and discover what it was he must do. The vicar's appearance, and the Anglican drone of his voice, were the first things which connected at all with the world in which he lived. This man, though using an intonation that he disliked, and probably affected by Popishness, was nevertheless by profession a man of God. Bryan's dull eyes lightened for a minute: here perhaps he might find what he wanted to know.

"I wish to ask this witness some questions," he said in a loud and arrogant voice. He did not mean to be either loud or arrogant; the harsh noise was the result of nervousness. It had not been easy to raise courage enough to intervene.

"Certainly," said the judge, not wholly pleased.

"What is the name of your church?" asked Bryan.

"St. Michael and All Angels."

Bryan frowned: the title was too fancy.

"What sort of service do you give in it?"

"I beg your pardon?"

"I mean: is it High church, Low church, or what?"

"I fail to see… well, anyway, I suppose you would call it rather High."

Bryan's face darkened. This seemed like a wolf in sheep's clothing. The man probably called himself a priest. A purveyor of corrupt religion was worse than an atheist. He must press on.

"Why did Mrs. van Beer cease to frequent your church?"

The vicar, who had resented both Bryan's expression and tone, snapped back, "Really, I cannot say. I don't see the point of this."

"Will you answer my question, please?" repeated Bryan.

The judge was impatient at what seemed to him random questioning. "I think," he intervened, "that this matter has been fairly well probed—"

A pale reflection of the rages that once alarmed his family flickered through Bryan's mind. Was he to be prevented by sinful and blind men from carrying to the end the inquiry which had been laid on him? He turned to the judge and with no diminution of his voice said:

"I must insist upon asking my questions. It is my duty to find out to my own satisfaction what was the spiritual condition of that household. I am to take my part in deciding whether this unhappy woman shall be sent to meet her Maker, and do you think I will be turned from my duty by a mere strip of mortality?"

The court caught its breath. Mr. Justice Stringfellow had never been called a strip of mortality to his face in his life. He let a few seconds pass in silence, and then with restraint said:

"You may ask questions dealing with the spiritual condition of the household, in your phrase, if you so desire. But you may not repeat questions which the witness has already said he cannot answer."

"Very well," said Bryan, and hesitated. Then he said to the vicar:

"When Mrs. van Beer ceased attending your church, she replaced the services by prayers in her home?"

"Yes," said the vicar, still wishing to make amends for his past failure of duty, "oh, yes. I am sure she did."

It was not till late that evening that he wondered what evidence he had for that statement, and reluctantly decided that he was not sure that he had any at all.

Bryan sat back and fell into thought over what he had learnt. Had he perhaps been allowed a glimmer at last? Could it be that this woman was one who was trying to follow the light? Had she gone regularly to church, and been slowly revolted by Popish practices? Had she then retired to her house, and in a pious and godly way, turned to Bible reading and spontaneous prayer? If so, it was nothing to her discredit that she was in the dock. For it would be her fate, as the fate of all the elect, to be despitefully used in this world. Was this the explanation? The evidence which he had heard and earnestly but ineffectively tried to retain fell from his mind never to return: he concentrated his thoughts on this one point alone.

Counsel for defence delivered his final speech. Counsel for the prosecution did the same. The judge summed up, at great length but clearly. Bryan heard nothing of any of them: he was waiting patiently but confidently for the answer to come to his single question. After the order, "You will consider your verdict," had been pronounced, he sat still and did not move till prodded roughly by his neighbour.

7

M R. POPESGROVE HEADED THE PROCESSION OF JURORS down a narrow corridor to the jury-room, as was his right as foreman. Behind him came the two women, Mrs. Morris and Miss Atkins; the nine remaining jurors followed in an untidy group. His face had a preoccupied expression. He had put the judge's summing up for the moment out of his head and was considering what should be his own action in the next few minutes. As foreman, his duty was to lead the jury and to make sure that justice was done. If his experience as a man of the world was any guide, it was probable that the first few minutes would be the most important. A turn might be given to the discussion then which would hang or spare a human being. Mr. Popesgrove closed his mouth in a worried line. What ought he to do? Decide swiftly himself what was true and guide the jury towards the same conclusion? He put the thought aside. The essential principle of British justice was that both sides should be heard and their evidence weighed in full by every member of the jury. It would be a failure in his duty if he even made up his own mind before all the evidence which they had heard had been dissected and commented on by the jury as a whole. The question was still unanswered as he turned into the room and took his seat at the head of the table.

It was answered for him by a juror from whom he had expected nothing but trouble. Edward Bryan's brooding look lifted for a moment from his grey long face and he spoke before any one else could say a word. His tone was less truculent than it had been in court, and more assured. "We have to decide to-day whether we are to project an immortal soul into eternity," he said. "I earnestly propose to you, before any one of us speaks or makes up his mind, that we should seek guidance, individually and in silent prayer."

Popesgrove at once approved.

"I think that what Mr.—er?—thank you, Mr. Bryan suggests is profoundly wise advice. Not all of us may wish actually to pray, but I am certain every one would be the better for considering in silence what he or she thinks of what we have just heard. With your permission, therefore, I will ask us all to be silent for five minutes by the clock, and to consider carefully what our verdict should be. After that, I shall ask individual jurors for their opinion."

A grumble of assent followed, and the room became absolutely silent except for the heavy tick of a large kitchenlike clock over the door. Bryan looked at Popesgrove with momentary hesitation. He would have preferred the interval to be specifically and admittedly for prayer. However, he had in essentials had his own way; he put both hands before his face, and prayed silently, making his mind as blank and receptive as he could. He was certain, now, that he would receive guidance and knowledge shortly. A slight tingling was running over his body, and the beginnings of an elation of spirit filled him. He knew these for symptoms: they made it sure that the light would shine upon him. He wished the space of time had been longer than five minutes. Light might come very slowly: however, he could but withdraw himself as far as possible from his surroundings. In a few seconds he had done so; with his hands before his face he was wholly alone, in darkness, waiting.

Most of the rest of the jury were unable to clear their minds during that brief interval. Popesgrove turned his thoughts chiefly to his own duties, which would be to suppress prejudice and to keep the distinction between what was and what wasn't evidence clearly before the jurors. Henry Wilson, the editor of a local paper, had tried to assist himself by working out how he would have written the story up if he had been reporting it. He had invented some good crossheads, but he found the device was in the end no good to him. He could tell what was important and what wasn't. He could visualize the makeup of the paper, and even the little patches of black type. But the STOP PRESS with *Jury's Verdict* in it remained wholly blank. Every one was making some effort at least to assemble his thoughts, with the one exception of Edward George, the trade union secretary. His telephone call at lunch had shown an even worse state of affairs than he had feared. Trollope and Colls had been struck, and the chairman had gone down to the job personally and delivered a violent speech. The National Federation of Building Trade Operatives had been on the telephone three times asking for him, and had left a message pointing out that the strike was a violation of a recent agreement with the employers which had been secured with considerable difficulty. The chairman had found the message, had rung up Mr. Richard Coppock, the Federation Secretary, and told him to go to hell. While George was sitting in the jury-room his union might well be being committed to a fight not only against a big London firm but against all its fellow-unions too. He had tried to follow the evidence conscientiously, but had been too worried to do so, and now he decided he really did not know one way or the other. Whatever the majority seemed to think he would agree to: that way it'd be soonest over and he could get away.

Dr. Holmes found himself in a condition of uncomfortable suspense. Out of the whole case but two documents had appeared, and documents were the only things which he knew that he could judge. One was the cutting from the *East Essex Monitor,* and one was Saki's story *Sredni Vashtar.* They pointed in exactly opposite directions. How should he decide which was authentic? Inopportunely, there came into his mind his favourite quotation from A. E. Housman, a passage in the Preface to his edition of Manilius:

"An editor of no judgment, perpetually confronted with a couple of MSS. to choose from, cannot but feel in every fibre of his being that he is a donkey between two bundles of hay. What shall he do now? Leave criticism to critics, you may say, and betake himself to any honest trade for which he is less unfit. But he prefers a more flattering solution: he confusedly imagines that if one bundle of hay is removed he will cease to be a donkey."

The applicability of the words was but too evident: he blushed in the middle of the silence and abandoned for the moment the attempt to think.

Two jurors, however, did find their opinions appear suddenly and sharply in their minds. These were the two women, the members of the gentler sex, as they had been referred to by Mr. Proudie; the two whom Dr. Holmes had thought would need his kindly masculine guidance.

Victoria Atkins, once she settled down to consider the question, knew at once what she thought. For what is it that makes the average man or woman unwilling to convict another of murder? Most usually, a surprise and disbelief at the action itself. It seems to any peaceable and quiet person so unnatural and improbable an act. He pictures to himself the process of laying poison, or of driving in a knife, and at once an immense repulsion seizes him. He knows that he could not do it, and he does not believe that the ordinary-looking person in the dock has done it. Give him one-third of a chance, and he will say "Not guilty," because the alleged act in itself seems preposterous. It is not done; it does not happen; it is not a part of the real world of newspapers and going to the office in the train. Any other explanation is to be preferred.

But suppose you had committed a murder yourself? Ah, then you know that that is all nonsense. Killing is easy, and the most respectable are as likely to do it as the others. Victoria Atkins reviewed the circumstances briefly and the facts became instantly clear to her. The van Beer woman had obviously scattered ivy poison on the child's food to get its money, and had trusted to the incompetence of the old doctor to get away with it. In some ways a clever idea, Victoria thought; it was far less trouble than that of choking Aunt Ethel. Nothing like so nerve-wracking, either. But after all nobody had found out about Aunt Ethel, whereas this woman had been caught by the police. Victoria consulted her conscience (if that be the word) on what verdict she should give. She reached an easy decision. When she was young she had been taught at the Home to be strictly truthful; old habits persisted, to the extent at least that she always told the truth when there was no clearly perceptible personal advantage to be gained by doing the opposite. She would say "guilty." In any event, the case seemed so overwhelmingly clear to her that she did not expect her vote to have any particular importance. She would only be one of a crowd.

The mind of each juror was like the dashboard of a motor-car or some other like machine. There was in it the equivalent of a dial with a quivering needle above it, calibrated for negative and positive—for Not Guilty and Guilty. In nearly all the heads, if one had been able to look inside, the needle was shaking uneasily about neutral. Only the closest attention could have discovered if the wavering to one side was larger and more prolonged than the other. In one mind, George's, the needle was dead still, fixed to neutral. The machine was not registering at all; it was disconnected.

Victoria Atkins's needle had swung right round to Guilty. So too had Mrs. Morris's. She had arrived at her decision more slowly than Victoria, and perhaps a little less firmly. But like Victoria she had been decided by considerations very far removed from the evidence. What had started her on her journey was, it is true, relevant to the case. It was a recollection of Mrs. Rodd's account of the death of the rabbit: that had decided her that the woman in the dock was the kind of person to torment a child and a dumb animal. But what had been final for her was the memory of her short married life. Why had her life been ruined and her husband killed? For no other reason then that murder was not punished. The arm of the law was weak: after Les had died the police had explained to her again and again that they had not got the power to arrest all the likely suspects and force them to confess. In Germany, and for that matter in the United States too, the law wasn't made a fool of like that. They fetched in everybody they suspected and if the guilty didn't confess right away, they were made to, all right. Over there they knew how. But here they couldn't even question people properly; and so Les was dead and not avenged. Alice Morris felt that by both sex and religion she belonged to the weak who needed protection. Death—unpunished killing—was too common and too near. Let the wall be high, the guns heavy, the defenders many, and above all let them shoot first at any disturbers and inquire afterwards. Les was gone; nothing would bring him back from the grave. But there were others, weren't there? Alice Morris remembered a hot Sunday afternoon and a desolate East End street. The needle in her mind swung round to Guilty.

At that moment Mr. Popesgrove shifted back his chair and cleared his throat. All down the table there came the same sort of shuffling, blowing, and relieved fidgeting as occurs when the presiding master finishes an overlong grace at school dinner. Only Mr. Bryan did not move, but kept his face in his hands. Mr. Popesgrove looked at him inquiringly, but as he said nothing decided to pay no attention. He turned to Victoria Atkins:

"Well, the five minutes is up now, and I think we should proceed. Can I have your opinion first, Miss Atkins—that is, if you have formed one?"

Miss Atkins's face had a disagreeable expression. Her lips were held closely together. Her eyes were invisible behind gleaming glasses and her pressed down black hair looked like a wig. "I certainly have," she said, and her voice was slum overlaid by servants' gentility. "It seems to me there's no doubt at all, and we ought to have done with this matter very quickly and be able to get off home. The boy was poisoned with ivy leaves: no one thinks it really was an accident. The woman bought the paper which showed her how to do it, she gets a fortune from his dying, and she was in the room when the poisoning must have been done.

The lawyer for the Crown said very rightly, to my thinking, that you can't have anything surer, short of catching her actually putting the poison in the salad. And that's a thing what never happens—people don't choose a time when they're being watched to commit murder. All that the defence lawyer said was imagination, not facts. It's perfectly true, as he said, that if we have any doubts we should refuse to convict. But the judge said that had to be *reasonable* doubt, and there isn't any reasonable doubt. She had the motive, the opportunity, the means, and was practically seen doing it. Well, as I said, short of watching her do it, what do you want? No question to my mind: Guilty, I say."

"Oh. Yes. I see." Mr. Popesgrove had not expected anything so downright. "Of course, if you feel so definitely it is very proper to say so. But I think there is rather more to be said than that. Perhaps the other lady may be less drastic. Mrs. Morris?"

Alice Morris had powdered her nose and arranged her face while Victoria was speaking. Half of her mind had noted what the ugly old woman had said, half had stared with dislike at the unaltering pair of eyes that always stared back at her from that shiny rectangle of a mirror, shaped like a pillar box slot, cutting off all the rest of the face that might give them meaning. Stupid eyes, beady eyes, too-much-seen eyes. Les had called them beautiful, all the same. She was ready and waiting when Mr. Popesgrove called on her.

"I don't see anything very drastic in what Miss Atkins says. I don't think women on juries should look at evidence any differently to men. I know we are supposed to be softer and more gentle and so on, but that doesn't seem to me to have anything to do with it. Actually we need the protection of the law more than men do, if anything; and I'm sure every one would despise a woman for letting a criminal off out of sentimentality. The prisoner is guilty, or she's not guilty, that's all: we must decide just that and not think of consequences.

"Miss Atkins put very well the important facts, and they all point the one way. I won't repeat them. I'll only add one point, and that is this. We have to consider the character of the woman. If she'd been very gentle and kind, I don't say that I wouldn't have had my doubts, and have gone back over the evidence to see if there couldn't have been any mistake. But look at what she was. I must say, I began to have my suspicions first when I heard about the way she treated the rabbit. For the child's sake, indeed! I never heard such hypocrisy. Think of her standing there, with the poor boy's pet deliberately crammed into the oven and screaming itself to death, and her holding the child back, and enjoying it all. A woman who could do that would be capable of anything. I wouldn't be happy, I couldn't face my own conscience if I let her go from this court with all the wealth that she has got by this crime.

"I think she is a very dangerous and wicked woman and we must protect society against people like her. I hope I'm not speaking too much about general things, but I feel it's specially important just now for every one to stand by the law and support the police. There's crimes of violence everywhere and the police haven't enough power. When they do act, they ought to be able to feel that the ordinary citizen, like you and me, will support them and not be led aside by any clever lawyer's speech. I didn't like that man and I don't trust him. I'm sorry if I'm talking too much. I vote for 'Guilty.'"

Here are the recording dials of some of the minds:

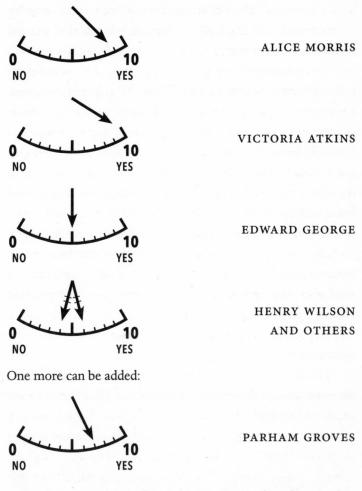

ALICE MORRIS

VICTORIA ATKINS

EDWARD GEORGE

HENRY WILSON
AND OTHERS

One more can be added:

PARHAM GROVES

Mr. Parham Groves, travelling salesman in encyclopedias, nearly a
gentleman, spoke without being asked. He was sitting next Mrs.
Morris, having planted himself near the only pretty woman with
expert speed. He may have imagined that Popesgrove would ask
him next anyway. He did not wait, however. There was nothing

he did more quickly and instinctively than agree with an attractive girl in whatever she said. In a world which mostly rebuffed and ill-treated him this helped to secure him the only triumphs that he was commonly able to win.

"I absolutely agree," he said. "That's very well put, if I may say so, Mrs. Morris. There is no real doubt about the facts of the case, and the woman's character makes the thing certain. You could hardly expect anything else. Look at what she used to be—a girl in a tobacconist's shop. She got into a state of society where she had no right to be. She was surrounded by money, when all she was fitted for was"—well, what would be most tactful to say? Some of these people looked rather cads, too. Better be careful. "—was something far different. Take that sort of person out of her class and you ruin her. She'd had some money, so she wanted a lot more. She'd got no sound solid core to her—no education either. And this is what results."

Francis Allen, the Socialist poet, had been patiently assembling as far as he could a Marxist interpretation of the evidence, but this was too much. "Nonsense!" he said. "That's the most ridiculous, narrow-minded baseless class prejudice." He spoke very loudly and his face was red.

FRANCIS ALLEN

"Gentlemen!" protested the foreman.

"Let me suggest," said Dr. Holmes, intervening with his most didactic lecture-room voice, "that we examine the actual evidence as dispassionately as possible, and without heat. I think it may perhaps be possible for me to be of some little assistance. My profession is one in which I have every day to estimate the value of evidence—a rather different kind of evidence, it is true, but still: evidence. I am a scholar, a Fellow of an Oxford college, as a matter of fact, and I spend my life largely in restoring the correct text of ancient authors. The manuscripts have come down to us in a very corrupt form, and, without wearying you with the details of my profession, I will merely say that in establishing the true text we have to estimate the value of many differing kinds of evidence.

"In listening to this case I asked myself: 'What evidence is there here which I would have to accept as unquestionably valid? What evidence would I class as suspect and second rate?'"

Dr. Holmes paused to clear his throat with a thick and rather disagreeable noise, and to assemble his periods for his next paragraph. By now he had convinced himself that he had in fact dissected the evidence as he alleged. If he had been more given to self-analysis, he would have noticed that his conviction had only become firm after his fellow-jurors had spoken. The last speaker but one he had considered a seedy, lower-middle class snob, a fabricated half-gentleman, a lounger in suburban tennis clubs who imitated the genuine Oxford undergraduates. He aped gentility and he should be put down. As for the women, they were certain to be wrong, and it was ridiculous to let them air their sparrow-like ideas before he had spoken. He had not much minded the insignificant and sour woman in black. She looked and spoke like a housemaid: she seemed to be that type of woman and that was the only type of woman which gave Dr. Holmes no offence. There had to be waitresses, and persons to clean out the Fellows' rooms and wash their stairs. It was bad management that a person like that should be on a jury, but at least she was not an object of disgust. Far other was the second woman, who was of course also screaming for blood, as women always did. Half-witted and with no sense of shame, she even painted and powdered her face in public when she was supposed to be deciding a fellow human being's life or death. She smelt of perfume: she was a reeking piece of sex, in fact. There was nothing Dr. Holmes feared and hated more than feminine sex. Since Alice Morris had voted for death it was fairly sure he would vote for life.

"I considered that nearly all the spoken evidence," he continued, "must be put in the latter category, that of second grade evidence. Spoken evidence anyhow comes to us through a distorting medium—the medium of the human mind. All of us lie to a certain extent, merely because the memory is fallible and never photographically exact. I felt this was particularly true of the witnesses we have heard here. You have the policemen—they are honest, without doubt, but they have their natural inclination to make their case sound good; and in any case what they said amounted to very little. You have the doctors—one quite obviously senile and the rest trying to put as good a face as they can on the fact that they were called in to cure the boy and only killed him. Poison, they cry, is the only possible explanation. Very natural, I am sure; but perhaps I am a cynical old gentleman. Certainly I am not convinced. At my age you suspect that sort of expert statement: you've seen too many of them."

"Aye, that's true, sir," said James Stannard, speaking aloud to his own surprise.

"You have a kitchenmaid who is far from intelligent, and a cook and gardener who are under very definite suspicion themselves. There is a newsagent who made a very poor showing under cross-examination and a tutor who made a worse one. And that is all the human evidence amounts to. A very poor and untrustworthy lot.

"The only evidence that we can rely on, as not having changed, is the documentary evidence. And there are two of these. One is the cutting from the Essex journal, one is the story of Sredni Vashtar which was read to us by the defence. These we can examine closely, and see what they mean. With them, we have at last come to solid ground. Let us take the first, the newspaper. It indicates very clearly that someone in that house knew that ivy dust was poisonous. That cannot be denied. But it does not tell us *who* had that knowledge. Nobody seems to know who ordered the paper in fact. That isn't very surprising, if you consider the matter a minute. Well over a year has passed and it's very likely that it's been perfectly honestly forgotten. Why should people have remembered a thing like that? What is certain, indeed, is only that that paper was in the house and any one may have read it and made his own deduction from it. Any one, including the boy.

"Now, the Sredni Vashtar story does carry us a little further. I cannot agree with the speaker who despises Sir Isambard Burns, the counsel for the defence. I think he has helped us very considerably. He may have prevented a grave miscarriage of justice. For with the Sredni Vashtar story we have at last a pointer towards a particular person. Nobody but the child is involved; the story points to no other person. He alone selected this extraordinary name for his pet, and no one else in the house even knew what it meant. We do now: the story leaves us in no doubt. Sredni Vashtar is the avenger. He is the guardian of an unhappy lonely small boy, who is tormented by an unkind aunt under the pretence of having his health safeguarded. De Ropp—van Beer; van Beer—De Ropp. How alike the names sound, and how disastrous the likeness has been! You remember what happened to this Mrs. De Ropp, the aunt who also killed her charge's pet? Her throat was torn out. She was murdered, to the author's and reader's great delight, and the little boy was happy ever afterwards. This is a frightful story to have fallen in the hands of a morbid and unhealthy child anyway. When in addition he gives this name, this name which cannot conceivably come from any other source, to his pet, he has given incontrovertible proof that he took up the awful suggestion of that story. I haven't very much doubt that he did try to poison her and only succeeded in poisoning himself. Poor little fellow: life didn't hold much for him and perhaps it is better for him really. Anyway," said Dr. Holmes briskly, recovering himself and brushing aside sentimentality, "there's not the shadow of a case against the woman."

"That's very true," said Mr. Stannard who had settled matters by his own processes of thought. "The fact that the police picked on her doesn't mean a thing. Not anything at all." The police, he added to himself, were busybodies and made trouble. And not above cadging drinks for nothing regularly: blackmail almost. Try and trap you the very next day too into serving after hours, likely as not.

PERCIVAL HOLMES

JAMES STANNARD

Mr. Popesgrove broke in again, in case the discussion should get out of hand.

"And you, sir?" he said to the insignificant-looking young hair-dresser's assistant, Mr. David Elliston Smith. Mr. Elliston Smith had hardly a formed opinion yet, but he felt he must say something.

"I don't care for the behaviour of the accused," he remarked. "She didn't go into the witness box, and she could have. A straight-forward person would have done so. It means one thing, I say, and that is that she's got something to hide."

"I agree, I agree," said his neighbour, Ivor Drake, the actor. "There is something sinister in that. Her whole attitude seemed to me suspicious. I watched her throughout the case."

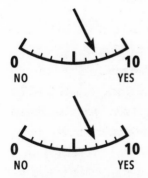

D. ELLISTON SMITH

I. W. DRAKE

Here Mr. Popesgrove knew that he must intervene and he did so effectually. "That, you know, we mustn't be swayed by. The judge made English law on that point absolutely clear. The defendant has the right to give or not give evidence as she pleases, and we are not to be prejudiced by her decision whatever it is. Many perfectly innocent people are unable to face the ordeal of cross-examination. They may know beforehand that they will make themselves ridiculous in the witness box and from sheer confusion and inability to express themselves rush into a mass of contradictions. Not everybody can keep their head when they're questioned by a clever lawyer on matters on which their life depends. If they don't feel up to it, they must be allowed to stand aside. Anyway, apart from all that, our duty is clear and has been laid down for us by his lordship in quite categorical terms: *we are not in any way to be influenced by this circumstance.*" He looked at the two young men with a mixture of persuasiveness and sternness. They abandoned their point at once: they had never meant it very seriously.

D. ELLISTON SMITH
AND I. W. DRAKE

Mr. Popesgrove turned to Edward George.

"You, sir?"

The trade union secretary started and said, "I've not decided. I would prefer to hear the opinions of others."

Mr. Popesgrove sighed with relief. There had been too much prejudice already—petty prejudice most of it. At least there was one man who was taking his duties as seriously as he was and was endeavouring to be impartial. The jury system was at the base of all British justice, and once or twice he had found himself wondering if in this case the basis was as sound as it ought to be. Here was a relief: there would be at least two just men.

If he had realized it, his own opinion was beginning to be formed for him. He had decided it was his duty to combat prejudice. A just decision; but prejudice in the jury-room was practically certain to be prejudice against the accused, and so it had been. The two women's speeches, the snobbish salesman's intervention, and this last exchange had all provoked him to defend the prisoner. He was finding excuses for her and already looking upon her as a person it was his task to protect. The needle in his mind was veering over towards acquittal.

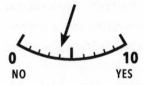

A. G. POPESGROVE

Before any one else could speak, Edward Bryan took his hands away from his face and stared at his fellow-jurors. His eyes were hard and excited. Light had come to him, and now he had knowledge. It was not easy for him to come forward and speak; but the duty of testifying had fallen to him and he would not hold back.

"I wish it had been open to all of you," he said, speaking formally but with obvious sincerity, "to receive the guidance and help that has come to me. Seek the Lord in prayer, and you shall find. I have done so, and as far as I may I will tell you what has been shown to me. I will try and use your own language, the speech of the market place, and I hope that each one of you will listen to me.

"There was in that village a house in which there was a great deal of evil speaking and jealousy. From nearly all who spoke there arose an odour of worldliness and of sin: they were persons, as one of you said, in whom no man should put his trust. There was only one person in that house of whom any good thing was reported, and that was the woman in the dock. The clergyman who spoke was a weak and vain man for a man of God. But he told us what was necessary: when she left his place of worship, for good reasons, she continued her prayers at home. She was seeking for guidance, and in that house it seems that she alone was seeking for guidance. The very fact that others in that house hated her and despitefully used her is proof that she was a righteous woman among the wicked."

Bryan hesitated and ran his finger round his throat, inside his stiff collar. How could he say to this audience what he meant? His real thought was: "All of you, as far as I can judge, are bound for eternal fire. I cannot tell whether you are more sinful or more ignorant; and I do not really mind. All the people in this case are in the same condition: impious, froward, uncircumcised in heart and ears. Except for one, the defendant, upon whom all the rest have made an attack. I was moved to ask certain questions, and, despite the obstruction of the judge, I learnt from them that she perhaps might be a child of light. You do not even know what that means. But I see now, that I was sent for a purpose on to this jury and it was to save a servant of the Lord in great distress. It was the Prince of Darkness who spoke through the mouth of the judge and tried to prevent me from asking the one important question. It is my duty to see that this woman goes free: that task has been laid on me by the Almighty, and all that you have to do is to obey."

It was useless to say this, yet he felt that without it his words were weak and ineffective. He was trying to argue, and argument was something he was almost unable to handle. He feared that he was losing his battle—that the jurors' minds were wandering away from what he was saying. In his mind he said a brief prayer for aid and pledged all his strength of will and his weak powers of thought. Refreshed, he put up his hand and stopped an interruption from Dr. Holmes.

"One of you," he said, "remarked that above all we must think of the character of the accused. Indeed we must. Violence and darkness surround us, as again one of you has said, and we must here as everywhere else seek to know who is on the side of righteousness. We are like the king who was sent by the Lord into Samaria when it was ruled by the wicked woman: we must cry out: 'Who is on our side? Who?' Who then in that house was on the side of righteousness? Was it the cook and the gardener, coveting wealth, besotting themselves with strong drink, and thieving? Was it the teacher of profane knowledge, with his hands picking among the books belonging to other persons? Was it the poor boy himself, cut off in his sins? Child though he was, he was meditating murder. He had been reading a book placed in his way by the Devil, and teaching him to imagine evil. Only one person remembered her Creator in prayer. What if she did restrain the child from self-indulgence? The world would be a better place if children were taught, as they were once, to value fleshly amusements less. We are told: whom the Lord loveth, He chasteneth. Will you blame her if she tried to follow that example?"

Bryan's vehemence of tone made up for the repetitive nature of his words. His almost colourless grey eyes protruded; he pushed his head forward in his anxiety and his long knobbly neck rippled like a tortoise's. The jurors paid him attention, though only Mr.

Stannard considered his arguments were of weight. The rest admitted that he indeed had a profound conviction, but they were not certain why.

EDWARD BRYAN

He stopped, and there was a momentary silence. Then Mr. Popesgrove realized that the time had come when he must speak, and that in the fine confusion of opinion that had shown itself the fate of the prisoner might well depend on what he said.

8

T HE COURT WAS ONLY PARTLY EMPTY. THE OFFICIAL ELE-
ment was represented by the clerk of assize and several
policemen. The judge, the lawyers, the accused, the jury were
all away. But a good half of the audience was keeping its seats,
unwilling to risk missing the verdict. It was pretty quiet, for the
possibilities of the verdict had been gone over so often that every
one was tired of prophesying. Several people were openly yawning and from time to time one or two would get up and go out.
The air was stale and the room was cold. Near the front a woman
complained of it.

"It'd be worse in America," answered her companion, a middle-
aged woman in a dull green coat. "Everybody smokes there. They
have spittoons in court, too, you know."

"I shall go to sleep soon," said the first woman, paying no
attention. "How long do you think it'll be?"

"No idea."

★

Mr. Proudie was eating two grilled chops and drinking half a
bottle of claret, in a great hurry. He had arranged to be notified
as soon as the jury moved, but it unsettled him to know that he
might be disturbed. He gulped his food and paid no attention to
the taste. The judge was in his room sitting with his eyes almost
shut. He was not asleep, but the habit of nearly closing his eyes
had become second nature. Originally he had encouraged it
because he felt it increased his formidability and his appearance

of wisdom. He thought of himself as sitting up there on the bench very wizened, very old and very wise, motionless and sightless and yet taking everything in. And then lifting his lids rarely and suddenly for a penetrating and fierce glance. Now that he had become a little tired of these vanities it was too much trouble to change. He seemed always to be almost asleep; well, it didn't matter, he thought, it would not be long before he would be wholly asleep, and for always.

Sir Ikey was in a nearby bar drinking hock and eating ham sandwiches. He had decided to have his dinner later and not spoil it by gobbling now. The sandwiches were made to his exact instructions, each was an inch thick, no more nor less. The two slices of bread were an eighth of an inch each and the ham was three-quarters of an inch thick, cut rather fat, for that was the way he preferred it. He had refused to go and see his client, telling Mr. Henderson that that was his duty.

Rosalie was sitting in a bare whitewashed room with a wardress. She had not cried, or made any sort of scene: the wardress thought her one of the most untroublesome customers she'd ever had. Sir Ikey had in fact been unfair to her. Judging from a very few conversations he had diagnosed her as incapable of self-control. But she had taken herself in hand more and more as the trial approached: it is probable, even, that she could safely have been put in the box. In recent years she had had no one to contradict her, and no reason to control herself. But earlier on life had not been so easy: she had known poverty when Mr. van Beer spent most of her allowance, and at other times had suffered various kinds of discomfort and humiliation. For much of her life she had been able to get what she wanted by nagging or flying into a temper, but not all her life; she had had to acquire a certain toughness which had remained with her. Once she had realized that temper was no good to get her out of this difficulty she found some amount of cold common sense to help her. She had had to look after herself in the days when she lived in Pimlico, she reflected, and she could do so again. Having money was no use now—that is, all its use was over when it had bought her an expensive lawyer—and making scenes was doing no good. It would have been a way out to drink, but you couldn't get a drop in prison. All there was to do was be quiet and sensible and cooperate with the lawyers, and that she had been trying to do. The thing was, she repeatedly told herself, to find out what was their line of defence and give them or help them to find all the facts that would help that line of defence. As for telling them anything else; well, that was another matter.

The wardress had told her she might smoke, and she was chainsmoking Gold Flake. Her hands trembled but she showed no other signs of emotion. When Mr. Henderson came in and sat down, she greeted him in a calm tone. Then she asked:

"How long will they be?"

"I don't know," he answered. "I'm surprised they have taken so long. But then I haven't great experience in this kind of case. My firm deals almost exclusively with civil law, you see."

"And—and what do you think the verdict will be?"

Mr. Henderson was prepared for that.

"We have very high hopes. Sir Isambard and I both think the same. We expect a favourable verdict. Of course there is quite likely to be some obstinate person on the jury. There generally is; and that would explain the delay. But I think we can confidently look forward to the verdict that we desire.

"By the way, Sir Isambard asks me to apologize for his not being here. He was snatching a little food. His speech was a great effort—a splendid one, I may say—but it left him very exhausted."

"I thought it was awfully nice," said Rosalie politely.

I N THE JURY-ROOM, THE LINES OF DIVISION HAD BECOME clearer. Five persons alone had strong opinions, and the struggle between them was likely to settle the matter in the end. Dr. Holmes, Mr. Stannard and Mr. Bryan were vehement for acquittal: Miss Atkins and Mrs. Morris equally fierce for conviction. The rest of the jury had no equally strong convictions: if one party were victorious over the other they would probably acquiesce without much resistance. This was true of all except Mr. Popesgrove, who had spent long enough, as he thought, in discouraging any partisanship, and now had made up his own mind. With none of the vehemence of language of the others, he was yet quite decided: there was not sufficient evidence to convict. He had indicated this, as he thought, when he gave his opinion before; but obviously he couldn't have spoken clearly enough. He must intervene again.

"There seems to be quite a sharp disagreement," he said. "I wonder if it would help if I went over the evidence again from the beginning? I made very full notes, and I have them here."

There was no objection, and he began his summary. He would put it pretty strong: there should be no mistake this time. He addressed himself chiefly to Mrs. Morris. She looked a little less obstinate than the grim woman on his left.

M R. PROUDIE HAD FINISHED HIS HURRIED MEAL AND WAS suffering the first consequences of having bolted it. He was also very annoyed with the jury for not having decided on its verdict in time to coincide with his finishing his cheese. To have hurried for nothing vexed him extremely.

The judge was really asleep.

Sir Ikey was walking about the corridors fidgeting and yawning.

The audience in the court had dwindled to twenty.

Mrs. van Beer and Mr. Henderson were sitting facing each other, having exhausted their conversation. Mrs. van Beer was showing signs of frayed nerves, and had begun to mutter under her breath. Once she said aloud, "Blast their silly eyes," and did not apologize. Mr. Henderson was becoming nervous, as he always did at female irritation. A minute later he rose and said, "If you will excuse me, I will go and see if there is any news. Perhaps Sir Isambard will have finished his dinner. If so I will ask him to come here and talk to us."

"Well, I think he might," said Rosalie.

Mr. Henderson found Sir Ikey walking up and down.

"Is there any news?" he said.

"No, how should there be?" snapped Sir Ikey.

"Would you come and talk to Mrs. van Beer?"

"What for? There's nothing worth saying. No, I won't come."

I N THE JURY-ROOM MRS. MORRIS SAID, "WHY, OF COURSE, I
wouldn't want to hang any one who was innocent. I don't
see why you should think such a thing of me. It's only I feel we
ought—" She hesitated: what did she feel? It had seemed so clear
for a minute. It had connected up with Les in some way, but now
this handsome dark man had confused her. But she must finish
her sentence for every one was listening. "I mean we oughtn't to
let people get away with things; but then of course if she didn't
do it I suppose she isn't getting away with anything." Her voice
trailed away to nothing; even to her her last sentence seemed
rather silly.

Dr. Holmes exhaled his relief audibly, with a puff of wind
that blew a sheet of notepaper across the table. He also made a
loud involuntary noise, which discomposed every one else, but
didn't worry him at all. His method of life made such sounds his
frequent companions. As he rarely was in polite company where
he might have restrained himself he had gradually got out of
the habit of noticing them. He eventually hardly knew that he
made them.

"Now that one of the ladies had changed her mind," he said in
what was intended for a fatherly voice, "we are nearly all agreed.
If you can persuade the other lady, Mr. Foreman, our task will be
over. Perhaps she will not be difficult?"

Dr. Holmes's last sentence was delivered with a startling leer
towards Miss Atkins. The dago, he thought, had done very well

with the little piece, and it was his duty to help him a bit by charming the old girl. He felt encouraged by a grumble of assent behind him: the surrender of Mrs. Morris had decided all the waverers that they too were for acquittal.

Victoria Atkins looked at them, all set against her and trying to put her down. If the Matron of the West Fen Home for Orphan Girls had returned to life at that moment, she would have recognized the expression which came over her face. It indicated one of Victoria's sullen moods: there was nothing whatever to be done with her then (in Matron's opinion) except to issue very clear orders in a distinct voice and see that they were obeyed *immediately*, making it quite clear that punishment would instantly follow any misconduct.

"Don't talk in that stupid way to me," she said directly to Dr. Holmes. "I'll thank you not to behave as if I was a fool. There is no doubt in my mind and my verdict will be given according to my conscience. The woman is guilty. She was all but seen doing it. You can make me sit here all night if you choose: I shall say nothing else at the end. You might as well make up your mind to it now."

Mr. Popesgrove tried his hand again. "Of course you will follow your conscience, Miss Atkins. It would be a very wrong act for any one here to do anything else. But since the rest of us seem to have reached a different opinion, won't you go over the whole thing again and see whether you cannot change your mind?"

He recapitulated most of what he had said to Mrs. Morris, trying to stress points which he thought might appeal to Victoria. His performance was the poorer because he had no idea what these could be. She heard him out in silence. Then she said:

"I know all that. It doesn't amount to anything. The woman is guilty. There's no point your going on talking at me," she added flatly. "I *know.*"

The pause that followed was broken by Edward Bryan. The arrogance of the last sentence annoyed him. Should one woman stand in the way? And dared that woman say "I know"? Only he, Edward Bryan, *knew*: others might guess, argue, or fumble in darkness. What did she mean by making a claim like that? He fixed his angry uncoloured eyes on her, and spoke harshly:

"What do you mean by that? How can you say such a thing? What *knowledge* have you of murder? How do you *know*" (his voice rose into a high key) "what would drive a woman to kill, and what would hold her back from that awful crime? Answer me that!" He half got up from his seat and jabbed with his finger at her. He felt rising again one of those long-forgotten angers that he had had before he had seen the light. But this time it was not an earthly and a sinful rage: he was on the work of the Almighty and he must not let himself be frustrated. In a slightly milder but none the less fierce voice he repeated the phrase which had sounded effective when he said it:

"What *knowledge* have you of murder?"

Victoria flinched visibly. She could deal with most things, but this wild man, with his staring fish eyes and his nasty talk about religion, like the old chaplain, scared her proper. He looked half-mad, and loonies knew a lot of things by instinct. Him there jabbing his finger at her and asking what she knew about murder, in that suggestive way! He *couldn't* know anything. All that was over long ago. But suppose he did! You never knew with loonies. Victoria felt herself begin to perspire, and had a strong wish to get out of the limelight as quickly as possible. What did this woman matter one way or the other after all?

She dabbed her mouth with her handkerchief and after a few seconds was able to speak.

"Well, I don't suppose I *know* anything, if you put it that way," she said grudgingly. "I only meant—oh, well, it doesn't matter. If you're all agreed, I won't stand out."

"Thank you, Miss Atkins." Mr. Popesgrove's tone was respectful, and grave. "I think we *are* agreed. Are we not? May I record a vote of *Not guilty*?"

"Not guilty," repeated the jurors in various tones and irregular time.

PART IV
Postscript

"LET ME DRIVE YOU TO YOUR HOTEL," SAID SIR IKEY TO Rosalie with his usual exaggeratedly deep bow. "And perhaps I can give you a lift too, Henderson?"

Mr. Henderson accepted briefly, but Rosalie simpered with only half-feigned embarrassment. "It's too kind of you, Sir Isambard; after being so good to me and just really saving my life and me being so difficult, it's really more than you should trouble to, really it is." (She pronounced her favourite adverb as usual, as if it were spelt with a double ee.) "You see the fact is, me being taken up so suddenly, and then being in there ever since, I've not exactly got a place to go to. Even if I wanted to go back to the house after all that's passed, which I wouldn't, I couldn't start going there at this time of night."

"We must find you an hotel, dear lady. How stupid of me." Sir Ikey reproached himself in the key of a very large funeral bell. "I expect you will prefer a quiet one."

"Yes," said Rosalie, pleased to have her feelings appreciated. "Like the Regent Palace."

"So be it," Sir Ikey began to say, but Mr. Henderson intervened. "The Regent Palace is rather bright and crowded; I think you would like somewhere more quiet," he affirmed.

Rosalie was still used to being given instructions: she had not yet realized she was free. "Yes, Mr. Henderson," she agreed dutifully, and thought for a minute. "There's an hotel called the Great Northern at King's Cross: do you think we could go there?

It's awfully quiet and is right by the trains. I do like trains: always have done since I was a kid."

"Why, certainly," said Sir Ikey, gave an order, and his big car moved smoothly off.

For several minutes Rosalie said nothing whatever. Then with the suddenness of a child falling into water she spoke.

"There's something I ought to tell you. Two things, really, I suppose. I've been worrying for a long time whether I shouldn't tell you, one way and another: but I decided not to, and of course it's been all right in the end. Of course I know you ought to tell everything to the lawyers but I hope Mr. Henderson won't mind me saying that he's, well, he's just the tiniest bit stuffy and as this might be looked on badly by some people in the end I said to myself least said soonest mended and that was all.

"Well, I don't seem to be able to get anything out, do I? Just say what you've got to say and be done with it: that's always best, I know. But there."

She paused in obvious embarrassment. Sir Ikey's monocle was glinting in the passing lights of the shops; his face was in darkness but he appeared amused. Mr. Henderson felt that he knew what novelists meant when they write "His heart turned to stone in his breast." He was afraid he was about to hear the particular confession which was the thing he least wanted to hear in the world. He had a highly disagreeable constricting pain in his chest.

Rosalie at last went on.

"Well, first there's that Essex paper—the cutting, you know. I did know about it because I ordered it, but as the newsagent couldn't remember there was no point in mentioning it, was there? It was just like Mr. Proudie said: I saw the story in the *Daily Mail* which only had a short bit about it and I said to myself, 'Well, that is a queer do; I'd like to read more about that.' I always was very fond of reading about crimes, you see, and every month I'd go into Exeter and get the *Illustrated Police News,* four issues all together, and a pile of those nice American magazines—they knew to keep for me *Peppy Detective* which is the nicest, but I like *Peek* too—but I wouldn't order them from Wrackhampton through Rodd, because it's not at all a good example for the servants and in any case those two were very much above themselves and thought themselves as good as me and it wasn't so easy keeping them in their places with Sir Henry's will being what it was, and I did *not* like them to know I read that sort of paper, not that there's any harm in it but they were only too ready to presume. I had trouble getting rid of them, the books I mean, at first, but after a while I used to cut out the more exciting bits that I felt like keeping and burn the rest down the garden in the incinerator. Well, now, I was explaining about this Essex paper: I said to myself 'I'd like to read more about that, I would,' and the right idea came to me very quickly and I said, 'I know where there'll be a full account, of course; in the local paper.' When I was in London, in South Belgravia you know, we all—my friends and I—used to read the local paper, the Pimlico and Something News, I think it was, because of the police news in it: twopennorth of other people's troubles, we used to call it. But that was easy said, only I didn't know what the Essex local paper was, and I wasn't sure where to find out, but then I remembered the Free, that is, the library, I mean: it's got a reference library too and I went into the room and I said to the young lady there, 'Excuse me, miss, but can you tell me how to find about local papers?' and she said, 'Local papers, ma'm?' and I said, 'Yes, to know what is the local paper for different places, you know,' and she said I should look at a thing called *Willing's Press Guide* and there it was in it, all quite clear. The paper was a weekly so it was quite easy to know what day to get. Well, I saw at once I couldn't get it in Exeter that day, so I thought why not order it through the man in Wrackhampton? After all, there's nothing wrong in ordering a local paper. So I did, and I cut out the interesting thing in it and burnt the rest.

"And as for how it got in that book, really I don't know. You can't remember everything after a year, can you? I expect that what you said to me was right, only you didn't know it was me. I must have been reading it one day and someone came in and I shut it quickly up in a book—maybe it was Philip came in and I didn't want him to see me reading anything morbid, or maybe it was one of the Rodds with their spying ways. Anyway, I forgot all about it until I saw that the police had found it and it did give me a proper turn."

Mr. Henderson sighed his relief. This was nothing like what he had feared. In fact it was hardly anything of importance. But Sir Ikey would not leave well alone.

"I think you said that you had two things to tell us, Mrs. van Beer," he said. Gloom settled on Mr. Henderson again.

"Yes, I have; and it's really quite difficult to know how to put it. I've felt quite uncomfortable, I have, really quite often, with you working so hard at it and me knowing all about all of it all the time. You see, I know just exactly what did happen, and quite often I've wondered whether I oughtn't to say so. I do hope you won't think it was impolite of me?"

Mr. Henderson began to say, "It is quite unnecessary—" but he was boomed down.

"Impolite? Indeed not." If a raven smiles, it smiles as Sir Ikey did. "But I think both of us would like to know just what did happen."

"Why, I thought any one would guess. I went out in the garden before lunch, and so did Philip, but we didn't go together. And when I looked back I saw him scooping something up with his hands on the brick path, where the ivy dust falls. I said to myself, 'I wonder what that child is doing?' and just then he slips back into the dining-room holding something in his hands. So I stopped and thought for a minute and I said to myself again, 'I wonder if he's been reading about ivy dust and knows it's poison,' and so I walk back to the house, not hurrying or doing anything unusual, you see, so as not to let on if he was watching.

"And then I went into the dining-room, and there it was; I was quite right. The salad dressing was all full of gritty ivy dust sort of stirred in. Stirred in by someone's dirty finger, I daresay. 'Well,' I said to myself, 'that's the game, is it? Poisoning your aunt, Master Philip.' I thought a touch of his own medicine wouldn't do him any harm, so I stirred it in a little more thoroughly—I'm glad Ada didn't notice me doing that!—and said nothing about it. And we both ate it for lunch. However, after that I thought that it was foolish to take any risks and I went upstairs and put my finger down my throat and never felt any the worse for it."

The total silence which greeted this narrative rather took Rosalie aback. She felt that perhaps she might need to offer some further explanation.

"I thought it best to say nothing till now because—well, because people are so queer and unfair. Of course, the way it is,

Philip killed himself and you can't say anything else. But some people are so narrow-minded that they'd say me letting him eat it wasn't any better than murder. I really believe they would."

"You're quite right, Mrs. van Beer," said Sir Ikey. "Some people are so narrow-minded I really believe they would. And this, I think, is your hotel."

Also Available

THE POISONED
CHOCOLATES CASE

Anthony Berkeley

'All his stories are amusing,
and he is a master of the final twist'
AGATHA CHRISTIE

'One of the most stunning trick stories
in the history of detective fiction'
JULIAN SYMONS

Graham and Joan Bendix have apparently succeeded in making
that eighth wonder of the modern world, a happy marriage. And
into the middle of it there drops, like a clap of thunder, a box of
chocolates.

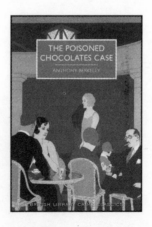

ISBN 978 0 7123 5653 4